BY MARTIN COPELAND

The Boys from Dogtown
LA Love Stories
Manhunt in Francde
River of Doubt
Right Proud: the Buffalo Soldiers

Memorable lives from Western history

LAME DEER

Memoirs of a Sioux Medicine Man

A Play in Two Acts

by

MARTIN COPELAND

ADAPTED FROM <u>LAME DEER. SEEKER OF VISIONS.</u>
by John (Fire) Lame Deer and Richard Erdoes

with SITTING BULL & BUFFALO SOLDIER

RAINBOW BRIDGE

ISBN: 978-1-7341123-0-6

Rainbow Bridge Books

CONTENTS

CAST

TAHCA USHTE, called LAME DEER, a medicine man of the Ikce Wicasa Indian nation.

NOTES

Readers who enjoy Lame Deer's memoirs are strongly encouraged to obtain <u>LAME DEER. SEEKER OF VISIONS,</u> the book by John (Fire) Lame Deer and Richard Erdoes from which this play is adapted.

—STAGING. The stage can be bare except for a glass case and a little dirt, or contain a replica of a sweat lodge, sacred peace pipes, silver rodeo spurs, a .30-.30 rifle, and more.

Or nothing at all.

We might hear the sounds of battle, the cries of eagles and owls, the rhythmic chanting of the sun dance. Or nothing but Lame Deer's voice.

Lame Deer can dress in a patched-up, faded shirt, jeans and down-at-the-heels cowboy boots or the traditional robes and bonnet of the Ikce Wikasa, or one or the other depending on the Act. Equally he can wear anything he wants: "The Great Spirit abhors people doing the same thing all the time."

LAME DEER

ACT I

CURTAIN rises.

The stage is dark except for a brightly lit glass case in one corner, the kind typically used in museums to exhibit artifacts. Inside the glass case is a 19th century rifle.

Lame Deer's voice echoes from the dark of the stage.

LAME DEER
In the Museum of the American Indian in New York are five or six "Famous Guns of Famous Indian Chiefs." A note next to one says it belonged to the famous Chief Lame Deer, killed in a battle with General Miles.

Tahca Ushte--the first Lame Deer--was my great-grandfather on my father's side. He was killed by mistake. You could say he was murdered.

He had made a treaty with the U.S. Government. They measured off four square miles west of what is now Rapid City, South Dakota. This land was to be ours forever--"as long as the sun shines and the grass grows."

The old people have told me that the prairie had never been more beautiful than it was that spring. The grass was high and green. The slopes were covered with flowers, and the air was full of good smells and the song of birds. If the Indians has only one hunt left, this was how they wished it to be.

Lame Deer and his people were enjoying their last vacation from the white man.

General Miles was stupid not to grasp this, but I think he acted in good faith. Nobody had told him about the treaty. He had six companies of walking soldiers and several troops of cavalry... more than all the Indians together, including the women and children. The blue coats came tearing into camp, shooting and yelling, stampeding the horses and riding down the people.

At the same time one of them carried a white flag of truce.

General Miles kept shouting "Kola, kola--friend, friend." It sure was a strange way for friends to drop in.

Nelson A. Miles

Peace was not what his soldiers wanted. They wanted Indian scalps and souvenirs. Probably they also wanted to get at the women and girls. The soldiers opened up with everything they had, killing Lame Deer, his second chief, and about a dozen other warriors. Then they plundered the tipis.

Even General Miles was not too proud to take a few things for himself, and that is why my great-grandfather's rifle is in a New York museum instead of hanging on my wall.

The lights come up and we see TAHCA USHTE--LAME DEER--an Indian medicine man of the Ikce Wicasa tribe, called by white men "Sioux" or "Lakota." He is an imposing man whose earthy humor comes from having lived hard and much and welcomed all life has had to teach. His spiritual wisdom reflects all his years since boyhood of studying men, the ancient ways of his people, and the world of his visions. He has been ruefully eying the glass case. Now he turns to speak to his listeners directly. As he talks, he roams freely.

LAME DEER

Maybe it was a good thing they didn't let us keep that land along the Rapid River. Think of what would have been missed: the motels with their neon signs, the pawn shops, the giftie shoppies, the Genuine Indian Crafts Center with its beadwork from Taiwan and Hong Kong, the life-size dinosaur made of green concrete. Just think: If that land belonged to us Indians there would only be trees, grass and some animals running free. All that real estate would be going to waste!

He shakes his head at the irony of it all.

LAME DEER

I'm called John Fire on some
white man's documents, but my
Indian name is Lame Deer, after
my great-grandfather, and that
is as it should be.

I was born a fullblood Indian in
a twelve-by-twelve log cabin
between Pine Ridge and Rosebud, South Dakota. Maka tan-
ham wicasa wan--I am a man of
the earth, as we say. Our people
don't call themselves Sioux or
Dakota. That's white man talk.
We call ourselves Ikce Wicasa--
the natural humans, the free,
wild, common people. I am pleased to be called that.

I am a medicine man and I want
to talk about visions, spirits and
sacred things. But you must
know something about the man

Lame Deer before you can understand the medicine man Lame Deer. So I will start with the man, the boy, and we'll get to the medicine part later.

My mother's name was Sally Red Blanket. She was good to look at, a beautiful woman with long, curly hair. She was very skilled with her hands, doing fine beadwork. She used the tiniest beads, the ones you can't get anymore. Much later, when I was half grown, I noticed that whenever a trader looked at her work with a magnifying glass or fingered it too long, the price went up.

My father was loved by everybody. He was the silent type. He used to tease me, pat me on the head, show that he loved me in a hundred different ways, but for weeks he did not say one goddamn word to me. Once I was thrown from a horse. I came down real hard. My father told me, "Don't kill yourself, son." It was one of the few things he ever said to me. That's why I remember it.

He was a kind, smiling, very generous man.

Most of my childhood days weren't very exciting, and that was all right with me. We had a good, simple life. One day passed like another. Only in one way was I different from other

Sioux chiefs on horseback—Photo by Edward S. Curtis

Indian kids. I was never hungry,
because my dad had so many
horses and cattle.

Like all Indian children, I was
spoiled. I was never beaten; we
don't treat children that way.
I was never scolded, never heard
a harsh word. "Ajustan--leave it
alone"--that was the worst.
Indian children are surrounded
by relatives as with a warm
blanket. They're rarely forced to
do something they don't like,
even if it is good for them.
They're so used to being handled gently, to get away with
things, that they don't often pay
much attention to what the
grownups tell them.

Now sometimes I feel like yelling at one of these brash kids, "Hey, you little son-of-a-bitch, listen to me." That would make him listen all right, but I can't do it.

Like most Indian children, my upbringing was done by my grandparents.

Grandma always got up early in the morning before everybody else, taking down the big tin container with the Government-issue coffee. She always made a huge pot, and then she kept the pot going all day. When the black medicine gave out, she added water and a lot more coffee and boiled the whole again. That stuff got stronger and stronger, thicker and thicker. In the end you could almost stick the spoon in there and it would keep standing upright. Grandma would say, "Now the coffee is real good."

My grandfather Good Fox played a big part in my life, and I looked up to him. He was a famous warrior who had been in the Custer fight. Everybody could see the scars all over his arm where he had been wounded by the white soldiers. Most of his war honors came from "counting coup." He'd ride straight up to the enemy, zigzag among them, and touch them with his crooked coup stick. That was his way of showing his bravery. Compared to my grandfathers,

we reservation people of today
are just plain chicken.
He was also a survivor of the
Wounded Knee massacre. He
told me, "Every time I hear a
lady or child screaming I think
of that terrible day of killing.
The preachers and missionaries
tell you to turn the other cheek
and to love your neighbor like
yourself. Grandson, I don't know
how the white people treat each
other, but I don't think they love
us more than they love themselves. Some don't love us at
all."

Lame Deer pauses a moment, then says softly:

                    LAME DEER
Wounded Knee...when the
people dared to go there and
look for survivors, they found
four babies still alive. Their
dying mothers had carefully
wrapped them in their shawls.
My grandfather told me about
the dead mother with a baby
nursing at her cold breast, drinking that cold milk. One or two
women were also still alive. They
had lain there bleeding, in the
open snow, for three days, in a
blizzard and without food. These
were strong women. One of the
babies was a little girl, Sintkala
Noni, or Lost Bird. They say that
she had a tiny American flag
made of beads on her baby bonnet.

Another pause.

LAME DEER

It was said that I didn't take after my grandpa Good Fox, whom
I loved, but after my other
grandfather, Crazy Heart, whom
I never knew. They said I picked
up where he left off, because I
was so daring and full of the devil. Crazy Heart was hot-tempe-
red, always feuding and on the
warpath. At the same time he
saved lots of people, gave wise
counsel, urged the people to do
right. Everybody who listened to
him said that he was a very en-
couraging man. He always advi-
sed patience, except when it
came to himself. Then his tem-
per got in the way.
I was like that. Things I was told
not to do--I did them.

I liked to play rough. We played
mato kiciyapi, the bear game,
throwing sharp, stiff grass
stems at each other. These could
really hurt you and draw blood
if they hit the bare skin. And we
were always at the isto kicicas-
takapi, the pit-slinging game.
You chewed the fruit from the
rosebush or wild cherries, spit a
fistful of pits into your hand and
flung them into the other fellow's face. And of course I liked
the Grab-Them-by-the-Hair-
and-Kick-Them game.

One day I watched somebody
pierce a girl's ears. Nonge Pah-
loka is a big event in a girl's life.
The man who does the piercing
is much admired. I saw the fuss

19

they made over it, the presents
he got and all that.

My little sister was about four
years old at the time and I was
nine. I found some wire and
made a pair of "ear rings" out of
it. Then I asked my sister,
"Would you like me to put these
on you?" She smiled. "Ohan--
yes." I just had an old awl but
thought it would do fine. Oh,
how my sister yelled. I had to
hold her down, but I got that
awl through. I was proud of the
neat job I had done.

When my mother came home
and saw those wire loops in my
sister's ears she gasped. But she
recovered soon enough to go
and tell my father.
(PAUSE)
That was one of the few occasions he talked to me.

He smiles ruefully at the memory.

LAME DEER
After I was six years old it was
very hard to make me behave.
The only way one could get me
to sit still was to tell me a story.
I loved to listen to my grandparents relating the ancient legends of my people.

Many of these legends were
about animals. Grandma told
me about the bat who hid himself on top of the eagle's back,
screaming, "I can fly higher than
any other bird." That was true;

even the eagle couldn't fly higher than somebody who was sitting on top of him. As a punishment the other birds grounded the bat and put him in a mouse hole. There he fell in love with a lady mouse. That's why bats now are half mouse and half bird.

I was happy living with my grandparents in a world of our own, but it was a happiness that could not last. One day the monster came--a white man from the Bureau of Indian affairs. He told my family, "This kid has to go to school."

My father was like a god to me and Grandpa had been a warrior at the Custer fight, but they could not protect me now.
I went to the day school on the Rosebud Reservation, twelve miles south of Norris, South Dakota.

In those days the Indian schools were really bad, like jails. We had to stand at attention, or march in step. Some teachers hit us on the hands with a ruler covered with brass studs. For days on end they fed us cheese sandwiches. Grandma would sniff at me and say, "Grandson, have you been near some goats?"

The Bureau of Indian Affairs thought that the best way to teach us was to stop us from being Indians. We were forbidden to talk our language or to sing our songs. My first teacher didn't speak a word of Lakota. He said, "Stand," "Sit down!" He said it again and again until we caught on. "Sit, stand, sit, stand. Go and stop. Yes and no." All without spelling, just by sound.

We also had a lady teacher. She used the same method. She'd hold up a stick and say, "One." Then she'd hold up two sticks and say, "Two," over and over again. For many weeks she showed us pictures and said "dog" or "cat." It took me three years to learn to say, "I want this."

The government teachers were all third grade teachers. They taught up to this grade and that was the highest. I stayed in that goddamn third grade for six years. There wasn't any other. Year after year the same grade all over again.

In all those years at the day school they never taught me to speak English or to write or read. I learned these things only many years later, in saloons, in the Army or in jail.

My teacher was a mean old lady. We counted many coups upon each other and I still don't know who won. I once threw a live chicken at her. Another time I fixed an inkpot in such a way that it went up in her face. They used a harness thong on my back that time and locked me up in the basement. I felt so lonesome I cried, but I wouldn't cooperate in the remaking of myself. I played the dumb Indian. They couldn't make me into an apple--red outside and white inside. From their point of view I was a complete failure.I took the rap for all the troubles in the school. If anything happened the first question always was, "Did you see John do it?" They used the strap on us, but more on me than anybody else.

I think in the end I got the better of that school. I was more of an Indian when I left than when I went in. My back had been tougher than the many straps they had worn out on it.

The schools are better now than they were in my time. The teachers understand the kids a little better, use more psychology and less stick.

But in these fine new buildings Indian children still are lonely. The schools leave a scar. We enter them confused and bewildered and leave them the same way. When we enter the school we at least know that we are Indians. We come out half red and half white, not knowing what we are.

My mother died of tuberculosis when I was seventeen years old. On her last day I felt that her body was already gone; only her soul was still there. I was holding her hand and she was looking at me. Her eyes were big and sad, as if she knew that I was in for a hard time. She said, "Onsika, onsika--pitiful, pitiful." These were her last words. She wasn't sorry for herself; she was sorry for me. I went up on a hill by myself and cried. For four days I felt my mother's nagi, her presence, her soul, near me. I felt that some of her goodness was staying with me. The priest talked about eternity. I told him we Indians did not believe in a forever and forever. We say that only the rocks and the mountains last, but even they will disappear. There's a new day coming, but no forever, I told him. "When my time comes, I want to go to where my ancestors have gone."

I told him, "That Christian name, John, don't call me that when I'm gone. Call me Tahca Ushte--Lame Deer."

With the death of my mother one world crumbled for me. My Dad turned me loose. "Hey, I give you these horses. Do as you please." I guess Dad knew what was in my mind.

I knew nothing then. Right or wrong were just words. My life was a find-out. If somebody said, "That's bad," I still wanted to experience it. Maybe it would turn out to be good.

I started trading my stock and bought things that were in style for the rodeo--fancy boots, silver spurs, gaudy horse-trappings, a big hat.

I hit the rodeo circuit. The riding suited me fine and put some cash in my pocket, but it was just an excuse to travel.

I trained myself to need and want as little as could be so I wouldn't have to work except when I felt like it. That way I got along fine with plenty of spare time to think, to ask, to learn, to listen, to count coup on the girls.

I did every goddamn, mad-dog thing you can think of--bulldog-ging, bronco-busting, buffalo riding. Those were real wild horses we rode, real cloud-hunters and sun-fishers.

You could be the first man to sit on one of them. You had to blindfold them to get them in a chute. Then it was hold onto their ears and away you go. You volunteered to ride the bad ones--"Bring on that man-killer"--just for that one girl watching you.

You had the wild cattle from the unfenced range for your steer-roping and bulldogging. In my day you went after that "rene-gade," roped it by the horns and rode your horse in such a way that it flipped the steer up and over like a flipjack. The flipping could break a steer's neck or yours. It's now forbidden, which is a good thing for man and beast.

The most exciting thing I did was buffalo riding. Those buffalo looked big and clumsy, but they went as fast as a dollar bill. They were real fart-knockers.

I guess the spirits were watching over me, because I never broke an arm or leg except once. I figured it was time to quit bronco-busting while I was in one piece. I became a rodeo clown named Alice Jitterbug. It was my job to divert the bulls from the riders who had been thrown, so they wouldn't be gored. I was dressed up as a lady with a big yellow wig and two pillows stuffed in my chest. I waved my red underskirts at the Brahma bulls to take their minds off the fallen riders.

Some times I had to dive headfirst into a barrel and let the bull bang me around from one end of the ring to the other. It was a little less dangerous than bulldogging, but only a little.

We Indians like to laugh. Our name for clown is heyoka. For us a clown's work--laughter--is something very sacred. For people who are as poor as us, who have lost everything, who

Rodeo Clown, 1940, by Russell Lee

had to endure so much death
and sadness, laughter is a precious gift. On cold and hungry
nights heyoka stories could
make us forget our miseries. We
call the heyoka a two-faced, ba-
ckward-forward, upside-down
contrary fool. He says "god"
when he means "dog" and "dog"
when he means "god." But he is
an honest fool.
He doesn't say, "If I get elected
to be a congressman, I will do
this or that."

Riding or clowning, it wasn't a
bad life. I slept under the grand-
stand, if there was one, or in my
bedroll out in the sagebrush.
And I seldom slept alone.
It was a rare night when a girl
didn't keep me company. My elk

power must have been strong. If my bedroll looked soft and inviting to some girl, if she felt like taking a short rest, who was I to say no, or to make her swear on a stack of bibles that she was single and had no brand on her. I figured that was none of my business.

Some men didn't see eye to eye with me on this. I got into some good fights. I told those jealous men: "Guarding an unwilling girl is like watching a sockful of fleas--hopeless."

At a dance on one reservation I met a girl and took her out to my hideout nearby. Then I noticed that I had left my coat at the powwow. When I got there I ran into her husband, pawing the ground and looking mean. Of all things he turned out to be one hell of a big policeman. He had his gun out in a flash and started calling me some very bad names. I didn't stop to listen but jumped on the nearest horse and away I went. He fired all six shots after me. He didn't hit me but one of the bullets hit the horse in the rump. Poor horse, he hadn't done a thing.

It was a sociable life, but also lonely, happy and sad at the same time. That was what I wanted. I heard a young Indian rider sing:

(SINGING)

"I ain't got no father
I ain't got no father
To pay for the boots that I wear.

"I ain't got no ma
I ain't got no ma
To mend my socks
"I ain't got no gal
I ain't got no gal
To kiss my ugly puss.

"I'm just a pteole Lakota hoksila
A poor Sioux cowboy
A long ways from home."

That's how I felt, except that
once in a while some girl kissed
my ugly puss.

I had many loves then. Even-
tually I got what I deserved. I
was married by force. The girl's
father was a big cheese, a
Christian with plenty of pull.
They put the pressure on me. I
didn't have any choice.

These people were Catholics and
I went to their church with
them. It didn't work well. People
paid more attention to me than
to the preacher. Some white
people didn't want to sit next to
me. After three years my wife
divorced me. She said I was
good during the day but bad in
the nighttime.

I was out of the trap. I hadn't
been ready to settle down anyway. I didn't want a job in an
office or factory, but how I could

survive in frog-skin land was something I would have to find out.

The green frog-skin, that's what I call a dollar bill. In our attitude toward it lies the biggest difference between Indians and whites.

Just before the Custer battle the white soldiers had received their pay. Their pockets were full of green paper and they had no place to spend it. What were their last thoughts as an Indian bullet or arrow hit them? I guess they were thinking of all that money going to waste, of not having a chance to enjoy it, of a bunch of dumb savages getting their paws on that hard-earned pay. That must have hurt them more than the arrow between their ribs.

The books tell of one soldier who survived. He got away, but he went crazy and some women watched him from a distance as he killed himself. The writers always say he must have been afraid of being captured and tortured, but that's all wrong.

Can't you see it? There he is, bellied down in a gully, watching what is going on. He sees the kids playing with the money, tearing it up, the women using it to fire up some dried buffalo chips to cook on, the men lighting their pipes with green frog skins, but mostly all those beautiful dollar bills floating away with the dust and wind. It's this sight that drove that poor soldier crazy. He's clutching his head, hollering, "God-damn, Jesus Christ Almighty, look at them dumb, stupid, red sons of bitches wasting all that dough!" He watches till he can't stand it any longer, and then he blows his brains out with a six-shooter. It would make a great scene in a movie, but it would take an Indian mind to get the point.

I made up a new proverb: "Indians chase the vision, white men chase the dollar." We are

lousy raw material from which to form a capitalist. We could do it easily, but then we would stop being Indians.

We make lousy farmers, too, because deep down within us lingers a feeling that land, water, air, the earth and what lies beneath its surface cannot be owned as someone's private property. That belongs to everybody.

We aren't divided up into neat, separate little families--Pa, Ma, kids, and to hell with everybody else. The whole damn tribe is one big family; that's our kind of reality.

My uncle used to tell me, "There's more to food than just passing through your body. There are spirits in the food. If you are stingy, that spirit will go away thinking, 'That bastard is so tight, I'll leave.' But if you share your food with others, this good spirit will always stay around."

I once heard of an Indian who lost a leg in an industrial accident. He got about fifteen thousand dollars in insurance money. In no time his place was overrun with more than a hundred hungry relatives. They came in old jalopies, in buckboards, on horseback or on foot. From morning to night a pickup truck was making round trips between his place and the nearest store, hauling beef and bread and crates of beer to keep all of those lean bellies full. The fun lasted a few weeks, then the money was gone. A day after

that the relatives were gone, too.
That man had no regrets. He
said he wished he'd lose his
other leg so that he could start
all over again. That man had become quite a hero, even to other
tribes, and he was welcome everywhere.

He pauses a moment before resuming.

LAME DEER
I was still young, a born world-
shaker, or just plain foolish.
There were still many things I
had to be. My life was changed
and I myself was changing.

Somebody tried to give me a
steady job as a ranch hand. I
told him I wasn't through roaming yet.

A fellow told me that spud-pi-
ckers were needed in Nebraska.
I used my last ten frog-skins as
a down payment on a broken-
down jalopy and chug-chugged
south. That first day I picked
seventy-five bushels and almost
broke my back. That farmer
didn't feed us; we had to eat raw
potatoes and sleep in the hay-
loft. I became a champion spud
picker. I learned something
about farmers and potatoes;
time to try something else.

One day I was wandering aim-
lessly when a white woman
came up to me and asked could
I do some sheepherding. Her
husband had been out in the

hills a long time now, taking
care of the woolies, and she was
growing kind of hot for him to
come back.

So for a few months here I was,
a Sioux Indian, a flock-master,
herding sheep a long way off in
the unfenced country. In the
morning I filled my cowboy hat
with water and let the dogs
drink from it, because I was told
that's what a proper sheepher-
der does. I was happy to be
alone, closing my eyes, thinking,
figuring, letting the spirits come
to me. But after about a month I
began to get restless. I got tired
of hearing nothing but the blea-
ting of sheep.

Day after day went by without
my seeing another human being
or hearing a human voice. I
used to go out and holler just to
hear my own voice. Those yel-
low-eyed sheep watched me.
They thought I had gone crazy.

There was no radio, but I found
a Bible and I studied that. So
my English and my reading im-
proved with time. "And Shem
begat Uz, and Uz begat Lud, and
Lud begat Mash, and Mash begat Nush." Begat, begat, begat!
Those ancient Hebrews, with all
that begatting, who in hell was
watching their sheep?

When the lady and her husband
finally came out one day in their
rattling wagon to see if I was

still alive I told them I'd better
quit before I forgot how to talk,
before I got married to a lady
sheep. I felt very sociable for
awhile after this, and my money
was soon gone.

One day some men told me,
"There's a new, powerful medicine. It's going to whirl you
around. It will make you see
God." I wanted to experience
this and I went to their first
meeting in a lonely shack. They
had a half-gallon can full of cut-
up peyote. "Eat this and you will
see a new light!"

The peyote was powerful. By
midnight I was having visions.
My eyes were on the logs. I saw
something crawling out between
the chinks. It was a big ant,
maybe ten feet high, the biggest
ant there ever was, all horns,
shiny like a lobster. I saw insects starting to eat me. The
leader whirled his gourd
around, shook his fan of feathers at me. I came back to life.
I was shook up. Something had
happened that I could not explain. It would take a long time
to think about it. I made a
prayer to the Great Spirit to help
me, show me. The men had told
me, "Eat this and you will see
God," but I did not see God. I
took peyote for six years. After
that I quit it. I found out that it
was not my way. Peyote is for
poor people. It helps them get
out of their despair.

Figure 8. "Peyote Ceremony" by Woodrow Crumbo (Creek-Potawatomi). The participants in the peyote meeting are seated inside a tipi; in the center is the altar, with radiating representations of water bird feathers.
Thomas Gilcrease Institute of American History and Art, Tulsa, OK

I had found out what a real Sioux vision is like. Once you have experienced the real thing you will never be satisfied with something else. It will be all or nothing for you then.

In a way I was always hopping back and forth across the boundary line of the mind.
For three years I was a bootlegger. I ran a little café and pool hall, with a dice table and a nickelodeon. I had the best red-eye anywhere.

Being a kind of two-face, I then wanted to find out how it looked from the other side. When there was an opening for a tribal policeman in the Black Pipe district, I went for it. I was surprised when they gave it
to me, because I was a hell-raiser, but I was popular with the people.

Right on my first day as a law-
man, I found out how it felt to
have a drunk cuss the shit out
of you. I was known as the rela-
tionship cop; everybody was my
relative. Now when your cousin
gets drunk you don't arrest him;
you take him home. I followed
that policy. When I saw a drunk
I told him, "Cousin, I am a real
mean man. Instead of taking
you to jail, I take you to your old
woman, let her use the rolling
pin on you. That's how mean I
am."

When I saw a young squaw
hanging around with the wrong
buck, I took her aside. "Say, my
girl, let me take you home to
your man. That man is no good.
He has a half-dozen girls already. He only wants to get you in
the family way."

"How do you know?"

"Because I do that myself. One
son-of-a-bitch with the squaw
fever can recognize another."

After I turned in my badge, I
think the drunks began to miss
me, but I wouldn't stay put in
one place.

I roamed the country on foot like
a hippie, sleeping in haystacks
or under the stars on the open
prairie. I joined five or six different churches, worked at
many jobs.

I didn't need a house then or a pasture. Somewhere there would be a cave, a crack in the rocks, where I could hole up during a rain. I wanted the plants and the stones to tell me their secrets. I talked to them. I was like a part of the earth.

I hardly recognized myself any more. Now and then, in some place or other, I looked at my face in a mirror to remind myself who I was. Poverty, hardship, laughter, shame, adventure--I wanted to experience them all. I wanted to lead many lives, finding out who I was. I was neither sad nor happy. I just was.

Being a good medicine man means being right in the midst of the turmoil, not shielding yourself from it. It means experiencing life in all its phases. It means not being afraid of cutting up and playing the fool now and then. That's sacred too.

Sinning makes the world go round. You can't be so stuck up, so inhuman that you want to be pure, your soul wrapped up in a plastic bag all the time. You have to be God and the devil, both of them.

A medicine man shouldn't be a saint. He should experience and feel all the ups and downs, the despair and joy, the magic and the reality, the courage and the fear, of his people. He should be able to sink as low as a bug, or soar as high as an eagle. Unless he can experience both, he is no good as a medicine man.

This period of roaming and cutting up lasted for nine years. I was a hobo and a hippie for much of the time, yet I felt the spirits. Always at night they came down to me. I could hear them. I could feel their touch like a feather on a sore spot. I always burned a little sweetgrass for them.

Always, after working at a white man's job or a time of hell-raising, I would go back to the old men of my tribe and spend many days learning about medicine and the ancient ways.

The years passed. I was getting older and had tried almost everything. I was like a big jigsaw puzzle. Year by year new pieces were added to form the complete picture. When I was thirty-nine years old my roaming came to an end. I settled down to my only full-time job--being an Indian.

I have to tell you about the time I got drunk and went on a big tear. I was with a buddy of mine. We had gotten hold of a bottle of moonshine. When we had finished it we were itomni--very happy, scouting for some excitement. We were thin-

king of how we could get
some more moonshine.

My buddy said, "Hey, here's a
car with no driver."

A very careless owner had left
the key in the ignition.

It was snowing, a real Dakota
blizzard; you could hardly see
the road. We didn't mind. Things
worked out real good.

On the road I met another friend
of mine. He took me to someone
he knew, an old white man who
took us down into his cellar.
"Gentlemen, what's your pleasure?" What he served us was
good--pure grizzly milk and rat-
tlesnake piss.

When the snow let up we got
rolling again. We made Cody,
Nebraska and traded a load of
baling wire for thirty gallons of
moonshine.

All that day we were enjoying
ourselves. There was a café in
town with a sign: "Ladies Invi-
ted--No Indians or Minors!" We
went in all the same, and that
started a big fight. We scraped
the enamel off some white pool
players who objected to our presence and counted plenty of
coups.

I headed south again. I think I
must have been drunk, because
I whirled that car around and

got stuck. We had to wade into
the town of Crookston through
waist-high snow drifts.

On the main street I came
across a Chevy, left with the mo-
tor running on account of the
cold, right in front of the pool
hall. It was too much of a temp-
tation.

My buddy said, "I'm going to
rest awhile." Chickened out on
me.

I was looking for a new compa-
nion but ran into the tribal police instead. "Hey, John, you
stole a Ford in Norris, South
Dakota. You're under arrest."

I just laughed at them. "See for
yourself. My car is a Chevy with
a Nebraska license. Can't you
guys tell the difference? Some
police we got here!" They looked
sheepish. They couldn't figure it
out. "Don't look so sad," I told
them. "Here, have a swallow of
bug juice." They had to let me
go.

I was on my own. Going east
was a little bit rough. The snow
was four feet high. But I still
had a pint of mni-wakan
to keep me warm inside. When I
got near Martin I left the Chevy
outside town. I figured nobody
would be looking for me on foot.
Night had fallen and I was
huddling in a doorway. I was in
a kind of haze but still sharp

enough to see the police fooling
with cars, checking the door
handles for fingerprints.

A young thing walked close to
the place where I was hiding.
"Wincincala, pretty girl," I whis-
pered, "come here." She wasn't
afraid of me or the dark. She
had her skinning knife out. No
wonder she wasn't afraid. "Say,
John, word's out that you stole
all them cars. Wow, you are
some warrior, some desperado.
Six cars!"

Six cars! I was dumbfounded. I
didn't know then that some
other man was loose on exactly
the same kind of spree, borro-
wing cars right and left. The police must have thought I had
some powerful medicine to pop
up in all those different places
at one and the same time.

Meanwhile, here I was getting
real friendly with that pretty girl.
"It's too cold here, John," she
said. "Let me take you some-
place and warm you up." She
took me to a half-blood bootlegger. This man was supposed to
be very sharp with a dollar when
sober. That's when his white
man's nature took over. But
when he got drunk, he was all
Indian with a sharing heart. He
was drunk enough then to open
his shirt collar to piss, as they
say. He motioned toward the
cellar. "Help yourselves. It's on
me." Then he lay down on the

floor and started to snore.

Boy, was his moonshine good!
Our clothes were steaming like
the hot pool in Yellowstone Park.
It was that kind of night.

Next morning I picked up a gal-
lon of bug juice so I wouldn't dry
up and found myself another
car, a brand new Chevy with
only twenty-five miles on it. The
pretty girl hugged me goodbye
and wished me luck.
I headed for Rosebud. When I
got back into Todd County a rider on a black horse was blo-
cking my path. Through the
whirling snow I could make him
out as a tribal policeman. There
was a .30-.30 rifle in the back
seat of my Chevy. Before he had
a chance to get his gun I had
the .30-.30 pointed right at his

chest. He didn't argue but threw his pistol down. I told him, "Hang on, Uncle," and fired a shot close by his horse's ears, and it took off like a greased fart on a lightning rod. I walked back about twenty yards and picked up the .38.

I made it back to Parmalee, where I had lots of friends, but none of them wanted to come near me. By the time I hit Norris, where my big spree had started, I was sobering up--a hell of a thing! I gave a man the new spare tire in exchange for five gallons of grizzly milk. I ran into the owner of the Ford, the car I had started out with. He seemed in a hurry to talk to me, but when he saw all the artillery I carried, he changed his mind fast.

After that things are kind of blurred. Somehow I made it to my cabin. I was good and tired. After all, I had been hard at work for three days--or was it four? Luckily, the first to arrive were the Indian police, Sioux men with an understanding heart. "Nephew," they said, "the white police is coming behind us. But we'll protect you."

They took me back to the road
and there, sure enough, were
about a dozen white deputies
waiting for me with shotguns,
rifles and pistols.

The newspapermen were all over
me, snapping pictures, telling
me to turn this way and that,
smile. It turned into a regular
funeral procession. I tried to
make them understand that I
was not all that dangerous, but
they told me that I was a desperate character and had to be
handled carefully.

My uncle, who was himself a
well-known medicine man, told
me, "Nephew, you are going in,
but there's a lesson for you in
all this. You'll come out of it as a
complete human being, so be of
good heart."
It was June when my case finally came up. I was two days late
for my own trial and they made
a fuss about it. "What do you

want?" I asked. "I'm here. I operate on Indian time. You people are always in such a damn hurry."

The trial was one big confusion. The witnesses contradicted one another and themselves. The judge threw up his hands. He was ripe for a nervous breakdown. "Please, Chief," he begged me, "please plead guilty to the first charge, and I'll throw out the other ten. Just listening to all this has given me one big hangover."

So I stood up very solemnly and said, "I did it, what it says in the first charge." The judge was so glad to be rid of me, he shook my hand over and over.

In jail I went to school every day except Sunday. There was lots of time to talk, to listen, to tell stories. One thing I learned was cussing and all the dirty four-letter words. That was a big accomplishment because we Indians didn't know how to curse. If a white man called me a dirty name, all I could do was to make the bear sound--hrrhn, hrrhn. But it wasn't very satisfactory because he didn't understand it. Now I could simply say, "You lousy son of a bitch!" It surely made social intercourse with whites a lot easier and less complicated.

Photo by Martine Marques

When I came out I had been
nine months in there. That's the
time it takes to have a baby. I
felt reborn.
I sometimes wonder what made
me do it, going on my big tear.
The nearest I can come to an
answer is this: In the old days, a
man could win respect by his
generosity, by his giving, but we
had nothing left to give.

One could win respect by being
a medicine man, but my religion
was being repressed and driven
underground. It was treated as
something shameful--a savage
superstition. I had to practice
secretly, if at all.

Once a man had been honored
for being a good hunter and
provider, but there was nothing
left for us to hunt anymore.

Bringing home the scanty Government rations, food that we didn't like, that was not natural for us, that we never got used to, didn't bring us honor.

We had been warriors once, honored for our bravery. Now we were nothing. In the past a man might have been born a cripple, but if he was clear-minded and thoughtful he would still be respected for his wisdom alone. But now our wisdom was measured against the white man's cleverness and we were told, over and over again, that we were stupid, uneducated, good for nothing.

We didn't want to be nothing. We wanted to be somebody. I felt that I was only half a man, that all the old, honored, accepted ways for a young man to do something worthy were barred to me. Just as there was a fence around the reservation, so they had to put a fence around our pride. Well, I had to invent a new way of making a name for myself, of breaking through that fence. I couldn't live on the glory of my great-grandfather, who had fought General Miles. Going on that joy ride was for me like going on the warpath, like counting coup.

I was young and maybe this was a childish way of saying, "Look, I'm a man. I exist. Take notice of my existence!"

I still can't help smiling when I
think of the big commotion I
caused. It had made me feel like
a man who was letting the world
know of his manhood. It had
made me feel that my living was
a matter of some importance,
that it had a purpose. This was
worth going to jail for.

He pauses a moment, a half-smile on his face, still enjoying the
recollection of his big tear.

Curtain falls.

END ACT I

ACT II

The curtain rises on a dark stage. We can just see Lame Deer
crouched down.

LAME DEER

I was all alone on the hilltop,
crouched in my vision pit, left
alone for the first time in my life.
I was sixteen then, and I was
scared. The nearest human
being was many miles away,

and four days and nights without food or water is a long, long time.

I wanted to become a medicine man, a yuwipi, a healer carrying on the ancient ways of the Sioux nation. But you cannot learn to be a medicine man like a white man going to medical school. Without the vision and the power learning will do no good.

What if I failed, if I had no vision? That would make me at once into a heyoka, a contrary-wise, upside-down man, a clown.

Night was coming on. I was still lightheaded and dizzy from my first sweat bath in which I had purified myself before going up the hill. As hissing white steam enveloped me and filled my lungs, I thought the heat would kill me, burn the eyelids off my face.

The medicine man had left a peace pipe with me. It had belonged to my father and to his father before him. Smoking this pipe would make me feel good and help me to get rid of my fears.

Darkness had fallen upon the hill. Blackness wrapped around me like a velvet cloth. It made me listen to the voices within me.

Suddenly I felt an overwhelming presence. Down there with me in my cramped hole was a big bird. I felt feathers or a wing touching my back and head. I trembled and my bones turned to ice. I took the sacred pipe in my hand and began to sing and pray: "Tunkashila, grandfather spirit, help me." Still I felt the bird wings touching me.

I started to cry. All at once I was way up there with the birds. I could look down even on the stars, and the moon was close to my left side.

I heard the cry of an eagle. It seemed to say, "You have love for all that has been placed on this earth. You are just a human being, afraid, weeping under that blanket, but there is a great space within you to be filled with that love. All of nature can fit in there.

"You are sacrificing yourself here to be a medicine man. In time you will be one. You will teach other medicine men. You will learn about herbs and roots, and you will heal people. You will ask them for nothing in return. A man's life is short. Make yours a worthy one."

I saw a shape before me. It rose from the darkness and the swirling fog which penetrated my earth hole. I saw that this was my great grandfather, Tah-

ca Ushte, Lame Deer. I could see
the blood dripping from my
great-grandfather's chest where
a white soldier had shot him. I
understood that my great-
grandfather wished me to take
his name.

Then I felt the power surge
through me like a flood. Now I
knew for sure that I would become a wicasa wakan, a medicine man. I wept, this time from
happiness.

I was no longer a boy, I was a
man now. I was Lame Deer.

The lights come up on Lame Deer. His head is bowed. It takes
him a moment to leave his vision. He turns to his listeners.

LAME DEER
Am I a wicasa wakan? I guess
so. You've seen me drunk and
broke. You've heard me curse or
tell a sexy joke. You know I'm
not better or wiser than any
other men. But I've been up on
the hilltop, got my vision and
my power.That vision never
leaves me.

A wicasa wakan can cure, pro-
phesy, talk to the herbs, com-
mand the stones, conduct the
sun dance or even change the
weather...he listens to the voices
of all those who move upon the
earth, the animals. He is as one
with them. From all living
beings something flows
into him all the time, and something flows from him. I don't

know where or what, but it's there. I know. This kind of medicine man is neither good nor bad. He lives--and that's it, that's enough.

The wicasa wakan likes to meditate, leaning against a tree or rock, feeling the earth move beneath him, feeling the weight of that big flaming sky upon him. That way he can figure things out. Closing his eyes, he sees many things clearly. What you see with your eyes shut is what counts.

The wicasa wakan loves the silence--a loud silence which tells him many things. Such a man likes to be in a place where there is no sound but the humming of insects. He sits facing the west, asking for help. He talks to the plants and they answer him.

A wicasa wakan is a man who feels the grief of others. A death anywhere makes me feel poorer. A young woman and her child were killed the other night on the highway. At sundown I will talk to the Great Spirit for them. I will fill my pipe and offer it on their behalf. I do this always.

He stands, begins to move around.

LAME DEER
Visions, a world beyond the green frog-skin world, have always been very important to us.

You could almost say that a man with no vision can't be a real Indian.

Out in the plains we get our visions the hard way, by fasting and by staying in the vision pit for four days and nights, crying for a dream.

The real vision has to come out of your own juices. It is not a dream; it is very real. It hits you sharp and clear like an electric shock. You are wide awake and suddenly, there is a person standing next to you who you know can't be there at all. Yet you are not dreaming; your eyes are open. You have to work for this, empty your mind.

Inyan Wasicun Waken--the Holy White Stone Man--that's what we call Moses. He appeals to us. He goes up all alone to the top of his mountain like an Indian, to have his vision, be all alone with his god, who talks to him through fire, bushes and rocks. Moses, coming back from the hill carrying stone tablets with things scratched on them--he would have made a good Indian medicine man.

All religions, all good beliefs, rest upon some vision. The trouble with white religion in America is this: If I tell a preacher that I met Jesus standing next to me in a supermarket he will say that this could not hap-

pen. He'll say, 'That's impos-
sible; you are crazy.' By this he
is denying his own religion. He
has no place to go. Christians
who no longer believe that they
could bump into Christ at the
next street corner, what are
they? Jews who no longer think
they could find God in a pillar of
fire, why would they go on being
Jews?

He shakes his head, pauses a moment, reflecting.

                    LAME DEER
To a white man symbols are just
that: pleasant things to specu-
late about, to toy with in your
mind. To us they are much,
much more. Life to us is a symbol to be lived.

He begins spreading red earth on a small board platform
elevated just enough to hold the design and allow his listeners to
see it.

                    LAME DEER
Here you see me spread some
red earth on the floor. I flatten it
with my palm and smooth it
with an eagle feather. Now I
make a circle in it with my fin-
ger, a circle that has no end.
The figure of a man is part of
this circle. It is me. It is also a
spirit. Out of its head come four
horns. They stand for the four
winds. They are forked at the
end, split into a good and a bad
part. This bad part of the fork
could be used to kill somebody.

If you look again at that circle

without end you can see that it also forms a half moon. With my thumb I can make twenty-four marks around the circle. This represents the twenty-four new medicine men who I was told I would have to ordain. Eighteen I have ordained already. A wise old woman once told me that I would die after I had ordained the last one. So you can see that I am in no hurry to do this.

(PAUSE)

Study my earth picture well. It is a spiritual design a man has to think about.

(PAUSE)

The white man's symbol is the square. Square is his house, his office buildings with walls that separate people from one another. The door which keeps strangers out, the dollar bill, the jail. The white man's gadgets-- TV sets, radios, washing machines, computers, cars. Boxes, boxes, boxes and more boxes, all corners and sharp edges. White man's time, with appointments, time clocks and rush hours--that's what the corners mean to me. You become a prisoner inside all these boxes.

I was once invited into the home of a housewife. "Watch the ashes, don't smoke, you stain the curtains. Watch the goldfish bowl, don't breathe on the parakeet, don't lean your head against the wallpaper; your hair may be greasy. Don't spill liquor

on the table: it has a delicate fi-
nish. You should have wiped
your boots; the floor was just
varnished. Don't, don't, don't..."
That is crazy. We weren't made
to endure this.

I think white people are so
afraid of the world they created
that they don't want to see, feel,
smell or hear it. The feeling of
rain and snow on your face,
being numbed by an
icy wind and thawing out before
a smoking fire, coming out of a
hot sweat bath and plunging
into a cold stream, these things
make you feel alive, but you
don't want them anymore. You
want everything sanitized. No
smells! "B.O.," bad breath, "In-
timate Female Odor Spray"--I
see it all on TV. Soon you'll
breed people without body ope-
nings.

It's no good.

Sometimes I think that even our pitiful tar-paper shacks are better than your luxury homes. Walking a hundred feet to the outhouse on a clear wintry night, through mud or snow, that's one small link with nature.

I knew an old Indian who was being forced to leave his tent and go live in a new house. They told him that he would be more comfortable there and that they had to burn up his old tent because it was verminous and unsanitary. He looked thin and feeble, but he put up a terrific fight. They had a hard time dragging him. He was cursing them all the time: "I don't want no son-of-a-bitch house. I don't want to live in a box. Throw out the goddamn refrigerator, drink him up! Throw out the chair, saw off the damn legs, sit on the ground. Throw out that thing to piss in. I won't use it. Dump the son-of-a-bitch goldfish in there. Tomorrow is another day. There's no tomorrow in this goddamn box!"

I was proud of that old man.

On all the earth there is not one leaf that is exactly like another. A human being, too, is many things.

The Great Spirit likes it that way. He abhors people being alike, doing the same thing,

getting up at the same time,
putting on the same kind of
storebought clothes, riding the
same subway, working in the
same office at the same job with
their eyes on the same clock and
worst of all, thinking alike all
the time.

We must learn to be different.

Let me tell you about some of
the herbs and plants we use in
our work. These herbs have
their own ways like all living
things.

Wina wizi cikala is a kind of li-
corice. It's bitter when you chew
it, but it is good against the flu.

Cante yazapi icuwe makes a fine
tea for all kinds of heart trouble.

Sinkpe tawote--that's muskrat
food, sweetflag. It has bitter
roots that are very good against
a fever.

Wagamu pejuta is a melon medicine. It's an emetic, a hot
flush; it cleans out your gall and
kidneys.

Badger fat is not a plant but
what its name says it is. It's a
good medicine against baldness.
Sage drives out evil spirits;
sweet grass attracts the good
ones.

We have many herbs that have
to do with child-bearing, with

baby care and with sex.

Hupe stola--that's the soapweed, a kind of yucca. It is truly a big medicine. Mixed with a certain cactus, it helps a mother in labor when the baby doesn't want to move down. Used in a different manner, it becomes a medicine which aborts. When there is a very good reason for a woman not to have a baby one gives her this. One uses this carefully after thinking about it for a long time.

Soapweed yucca

As for sex medicines, a certain kind of skunk cabbage, if you make a liquid of its boiled roots, is a birth-control medicine. It has to be taken with some care. Too much of it and you can't have any children. If a man is weak and can't get it up, a certain snakeroot could be a big help. One plant, if just a tiny seed of it is given an old man, can keep him going the whole night through.

I could go into the hills and search for a little plant with seeds all rolled up in a ball. You put two of these little seeds in a girl's drink or sandwich and pretty soon she'll scratch and bite you all over in a nice way. It acts on a boy, too. It will make an old man feel young again, real young. But I keep this a secret.

Can hlogan wastemna --a ragweed--helps a woman during a bad childbearing. It will also make a man fall asleep so that you can steal his horses, but it's no good for stealing cars.

A good medicine man doesn't pretend to be able to cure all sickness. A man who misuses his power in this way may turn witch doctor.

I never tried any conjuring of that sort, never wanted to. That's not in my vision. But I once played a trick on some guys, a stunt a witch doctor could have pulled. I was volunteering for the Army, going through my physical test. We were all standing in line being told to make water in a little bottle. There were many draftees there who really wanted out. They all said, "Oh, what I'd give to have diabetes or the clap. Then I wouldn't have to soldier." I told them, "Boys, you are in luck. I suffer from both, a social disease and sugar. For a buck apiece, I'll make a little water in all your bottles." Boy, were they eager, waving their green dollar bills at me. Of course, there was nothing wrong with me. I was as healthy as a bull. I was very busy next hour, drinking gallons of water, sprinkling a little drop of comfort here and there, getting more customers than I could accommodate. I made about forty dollars as a sprinkler. Well, that Army doctor was smiling from ear to ear. "I never saw a healthier bunch of guys in all my life. You'll all go into the infantry."

I had to take some of these new-made soldiers out for a drink. They were so mad at me, without treating them to a beer they'd have killed me.

I haven't told you all I know about the herbs and about the ways of our holy men. You understand that there are certain things one should not talk about, things that must remain hidden. If all was told, there would be no mysteries left, and that would be very bad. Man cannot live without mystery. He has a great need of it.

In speaking of sacred things I
will tell you first about the inipi-
-the sweat bath. I do this because we always purify ourselves in the sweat house before
starting one of our ceremonies.
Whether we celebrate the sun
dance or a vision quest, the inipi
comes first.

The sweat house is small, but to
those crouching inside it represents the whole universe. The
spirit of all living things is in
this hut. This we believe. The
earth on which we sit is our
grandmother; all life comes from
her. In the center of the lodge we
scoop out a circular hole into
which the stones will be put later. This pit is a circle within the
circle formed by the hut. This
symbol stands for life, for that
which has no end.

The man who acts as the leader
first goes into the hut with his
pipe. He covers the ground with
sage, which is sacred. The leader then burns some sweet
grass. One end is lit and the
smoke and sweet smell are whirled around so that it gets into
every part of the sweat lodge.
Thus everything is made sacred
and all bad feelings and
thoughts are driven out

Now all is prepared and the
sweat house is ready for the
people to go in. When you enter,
don't come in shorts or with a

towel around you. You are going
to be reborn. You'll be like a
baby coming out of your mother's womb, our real mother,
the earth. You don't want to be
reborn with a pair of shorts on.
If you come with that people will
think maybe you have something wrong with your dick. So
don't be bashful.

A man now brings in the heated
rocks, one by one. The man who
puts on the ceremony now lights
the pipe and passes it around. It
makes us holy and links us as
brothers.

The helper on the outside now
closes the flap over the entrance
and makes sure that no light
comes into the hut.
The leader now pours, or
sprinkles, water over the glo-

wing rocks. The water is ice-cold
and the stones are red hot.
There is a great surge of power.
You inhale that breath, drink in
the water, the white steam. The
heat is very great.

You sit there quietly in the dark.
You close your eyes, listen to the
hiss of the icy water on the heated stones, listen to what they
have to tell you--a little spark
coming to your mind. The heat,
the earth power, it hits you. You
inhale it, get filled with it. That
steam stops at your skin, but
the earth-power penetrates your
body and mind. It cures many
sicknesses--arthritis, rheuma-
tism. It heals the wounds of
your mind.
We open the entrance four times
and let the coolness in and the
light. Always we sing two songs
before we open the entrance
again. When the flap is open,
you might want to talk about
something, a sickness you want
to have cured. Or you might just
have to say something good
about sitting here with us in the
sweat house. Or some of us will
tell you that we are glad having
you here with us. Maybe somebody will talk about a drinking
problem in his family and ask
for help and prayers. It all depends on the reason the sweat
bath is performed.

After we smoke for the fourth
and last time, we say, "All my
relatives," and the ceremony is

ended. The last man to smoke takes the pipe apart and carefully cleans the bowl. We leave the sweat house the way the sun travels, counter-clockwise. We drink cold water and rub down our bodies with dry sage leaves. We come out with a feeling of well-being, lightheaded and happy. We know that we have done something good which will benefit not only us but all people, all living things.

We Sioux are not a simple people; we are very complicated. We are forever looking at things from different angles. For us there is pain in joy and joy in pain, just as to us a clown is a funny man and a tragic figure at one and the same time. It is all part of the same thing--nature, which is neither sad nor glad; it just is.

The sun dance is our oldest and most solemn ceremony, our greatest feast which brings all the people together.

Many white men think of it as an initiation into manhood, or a way to prove one's courage. But this is wrong. The sun dance is a prayer and a sacrifice.

The dance is not so severe as it once was, but even today it asks much of a man.

There are so many things to do,

or not to do, during a sun dance
that we always put one medicine
man in charge to see that everything was done right. This man
was the intermediary between
the people and the mystery power. At times I have been this
man.

The sun dance really began with
the choosing of the can-wakan--
the sacred pole. It was always a
cottonwood.

To find it the tribe sent out four
scouts, brave men of blameless
character. The "killing" of the
tree was done by four young

women who had never been gos-
siped about, who had never
been with a man.

The ax had to be brand new.
Each of the young women took
her turn, at first only feigning,
giving the young men a chance
to tell about their brave deeds.
Often this was done by way of a
song.

My grandfather used to sing:
"In a fight,
I yield first place to none.
Black face paint
I strive for.
Unafraid
I live."
When the tree was down it was
brought to the dancing place.

SIOUX SUN DANCE.

One thing perhaps we shall never see again: the mad rush of
the young warriors on their
horses after the last of the pole

bearers, every rider trying to be
the first at the pit where the
trees would be put up. What a
sight it must have been, the

strong young men milling in the
dance circle, the horses pran-
cing, kicking up dust, their
coats painted, their tails tied up,
the neighing, the snorting, and
yelling. War bonnets streaming,
the loose hair flying, riders knocking each
other from their horses in their
eagerness to be the first.
Those strong-hearted young
men on their brave ponies,
where are they now?

His emotions are strong, the memories great. He has to pause a
moment and gather strength before continuing.

LAME DEER
The actual sun dance lasted for

four long days. For the first
three days the men danced from
dawn to sunset, blowing on their
eaglebone whistles, their bodies
moving as one until they were
faint with weariness. And then
came the fourth, most solemn
day. Led by the medicine men,
the dancers made a solemn
march from the sun-dance tipi
to the dance circle.

Nobody had been forced or talked into this, but once he had
made a vow, he had to go
through with it. You can't break
your word to Wakan Tanka.

The piercing could be done in
four different ways. For the "Gazing at the Buffalo" way the
flesh on the dancer's back was
pierced with skewers. From
these were hung up to eight buffalo skulls. Their weight pulled
the skewers through the flesh
after a few hours.

The second way was "Gazing at
the Sun Leaning." The flesh on
the dancer's breast was pierced
about a hand's width above
each nipple and a wooden stick
or eagle's claw stuck right
through the muscle. At the end
of the dance each man had to
tear himself loose.

The third way was "Standing
Enduring." The dancer was placed between four poles. Thongs
were fastened to his flesh--two
in his chest and two in his back

underneath each shoulder blade. The loose ends were tied to the poles and the dancer had to struggle to free himself.

The last way was "Gazing at the Sun Suspended." In this case ropes were tied to skewers in a man's chest and back and he was pulled up into the air with his feet above the ground. This was the most severe test of all, as the dancer could do little to hasten the end of his ordeal by pulling or jerking but had to wait until his own weight finally ripped his flesh open. Some just kept hanging there until friends or relatives pulled them down.

Some white men shudder when I tell them these things. Yet the idea of enduring pain so that others may live should not strike you as strange. Do you not in your churches pray to one who is "pierced," nailed to a cross for the sake of his people? No Indian ever called a white man uncivilized for his beliefs or forbade him to worship as he pleased.

The difference between the white man and us is this: You believe in the redeeming powers of suffering, if this suffering was done by somebody else, far away, two thousand years ago. We believe that it is up to every one of us to help each other, even through the pain of our own bodies. Pain to us is not "abstract," but very

real. We do not lay this burden
onto our god, nor do we want to
miss being face to face with the
spirit power. It is when we are
fasting on a hilltop, or tearing
our flesh at the sun dance, that
we experience the sudden insight, come closest to the mind
of the Great Spirit.

Insight does not come cheaply,
and we want no angel or saint to
gain it for us and give it to us
secondhand.

Some of the outward splendors
of the sun dance are missing
these days, but the essentials
remain untouched. It is good to
see our people hold onto their
Indianness.

He pauses a moment before continuing.

LAME DEER
About this men-women business. The anthropologists are
always after us, wanting to
know about Mister Indian's sex
life. For years and years it used
to be "Who killed Custer?" Now
it's "aboriginal sex patterns."
One middle-aged, white anthro-
lady went so far as to ask an Indian man to undress and get on
top of her. She wanted him to
keep his war bonnet on, though,
and arranged for a third party to
take their picture. In the inter-
est of science, I guess. But the
Indian respectfully declined.
Some folks have fun with these
anthropologists. The game

works like this:

Anthropologist: "How's your sex life?

Indian: "Fine. How's yours?"

Anthropologist: "Do you always have the same position?"

Indian: "Yes, I've been an ambulance driver for twenty years."

Anthropologist: "You have a taboo about your organ?"

Indian: "The only guy around here with an organ is the Catholic priest. You should see him working it."

Some of our people are very good at this kind of thing.

Years ago I happened to be in the superintendent's office. The door opens and in comes a fat lady pushing a man ahead of her with a big feather stuck in his cap. She was talking a blue streak in Indian: "This man is no good. We been married for two weeks and this man makes love to me all the time. He just loves me to death. You must stop it." The husband says nothing; he just looks sleepy.

We had just got a new young superintendent, and this was his first case. I had to translate. That woman never stopped complaining; she just went on and on. "I'm in misery. The old goat is never done. We never sleep. What do you say, Superintendent?"

The Superintendent blushed. He started to explain: "In our white man's way we call this a honeymoon. That's when we have a big time. Consider yourself lucky. He has a husband's rights. Give him another try." I'm trying not to laugh, translating all this. I tell her "honeymoon," but it means nothing in Indian. She got real excited: "Honey, the moon, what has it got to do with me? This white man is crazy."

The Superintendent got redder and redder. He repeated it over and over in English: "Ho-ney-moon, ho-ney-moon." I told her in Indian: "That's what the white men do at the start--go at it all the time. That's what this honeymoon means. You've got to take it." She gave the Superintendent a dirty look and said, "If I die before my time it will be your fault." Then she pushed her husband out the door. "OK, old man, let's go and tawiton, tawiton, tawiton till we drop dead." You have a word for tawiton, but it's shorter.

You see, we don't have many sex problems here. When it comes to what you call the facts of life we are always very straightforward, don't tell any fancy tales to the children or lower our voices when we tell a sexy story.

But we have a great sense of privacy. We Sioux are real bashful, but bashful or not, we're no prudes. Looking around you, seeing all these families with eight, ten, twelve kids, you know that the people are busy at night, especially when they don't have that TV to take their minds off more important things.

Most Indian marriages last longer than white ones because we feel very responsible for the children. That holds people together. But we have our divorces too.

Having a child is always a great moment, like counting coup for a warrior. I am always hoping that there will be some twins in the marriages which I perform. That would make me happy.

You see, love is something that you can leave behind you when you die. It's that powerful. The nagi, the soul, it will roam and travel. If two people loved each other very much they come back again as twins. They had a great love, they're whirling around there, and the Great Spirit has pity and lets them come up again.

Some parents, if they had a child who died, a little one they loved above everything, wanted to keep its soul, wanted to "own the ghost." They would keep a lock of the child's hair for over a year, and then they would have a great spirit-keeping ceremony. They'd put up a spirit lodge and a spirit bowl with food for the little soul. For this day you saved up things to give away. You gave up everything, even the shirt off your back, not as the white man means it, as a figure of speech, but you really did this, because such a big give-away often ended with the parents handing out the clothes they wore. You gave till it hurt, till there was nothing left.

The anthropologists wag their fingers at us when we have a give-away feast. What they are trying to tell us is that poor people can't afford to be generous. But we hold onto our otuhan. All the big events in our lives can be occasions for a give-away. We don't believe in a family getting wealthy through inheritance. Better give away a dead person's belongings. That way he, or she, will be remembered.

If a man loses his wife, his friends come and help him cry. He cries for four days, but no longer, because life must go on, and if he cries too much the spirits will give him something extra to cry about. Not so long ago I saw an old lady who still cut her hair short to mourn for a dead grandson. After four days

she and her husband emptied
the whole house. They gave
away the grand piano, the TV,
even their bed. They were sitting
on the bare floor calling out to
the people who came to pay
their respects, "Say, brother,
sister, do you need this thing? If
it is useful to you, take it."

Only the empty walls were left at
the end of the day. Friends gave
them a new bed.

Our sacred pipe--I have left
speaking about it to the very
last. This pipe is our most sacred possession. All our religion
flows from it.

Crying for a vision, suffering at
the sun dance, in the sweat
lodge, the pipe is always there.

As we stand on grandmother
earth, raising our sacred pipe in
prayer, its stem forms a bridge
from earth through man
through our own bodies, to the
sky, to Wakan Tanka, the
grandfather spirit. As the pipe
is filled with our sacred red
willow bark tobacco, each tiny
grain represents one of the living things on this earth. All of
the Great Spirit's creations, the
whole universe, is in that pipe.
All of us is in that pipe at the
moment of prayer.

For us Indians there is just the
pipe, the earth we sit on and the
open sky. That smoke from the

peace pipe, it goes straight up to
the spirit world. Power flows
down to us through that smoke.
You feel that power as you hold
your pipe; it moves right into
your body. It makes your hair
stand up. That pipe is not just a
thing; it is alive.

Nothing of importance, good or
bad, takes place among us without the pipe. And the pipe has
to be properly smoked, every
person sitting in his right place,
in a circle, the pipe being passed
back to the dark
from the light in a sacred manner, because it is our altar.

A Sioux without his pipe is only
a half Indian, only half a man.

According to out belief, untold
lifetimes ago, the peace pipe was
brought to us by the Buffalo
Woman, a beautiful maiden. She
taught our tribes how to use the
pipe, filling it with red willow
bark tobacco and lighting it with
a dry buffalo chip.

She showed the people how to
pray with the pipe. lifting it up
to the sky, lowering it toward
the earth, pointing it in the four
directions from which the wind
blows.

After she had done all this the
White Buffalo Woman took leave
of the people. She was singing:
"Niya taniya mawani ye."

It means that as long as we honor the pipe we will live, will remain ourselves.

As the people watched, the
beautiful woman turned into a
white buffalo. It kept on walking
toward the horizon until it finally disappeared. This too is good
to think about, easy to understand. The buffalo was part of us,
his flesh and blood being absor-
bed by us until it became our
own flesh and blood. Our clothing, our tipis, everything we
needed for life came from the
buffalo's body. It was hard to
say where the animal ended and
the man began. When the buffalo disappeared, the old, wild, Indian disappeared, too.

In life and death we and the
buffalo have always shared the
same fate.

The pipe the White Buffalo Woman gave to us is still kept by
the tribe as its most sacred heir-
loom. It is called
Ptehincala Huhu Canunpa--
Buffalo Calf Bone Pipe. There is
also a second, very sacred tribal
pipe, one among the first made
from red pipestone in the way
the White Buffalo Woman taught
the people.

Only once in a lifetime, if that
often, can these two sacred heir-
looms be seen. I was one of the
few men privileged to hold these
two pipes and to pray with

them. It really changed my life.

One winter many years ago, I went north to Green Grass, where I heard the Buffalo Calf Pipe was kept. A woman was in charge of it, Mrs. Elk Head.

The going was hard. There was a Cayuse wind, blizzards, an icy cold. The snow was hard and shiny, like glass.

I went to a house in Green Grass where I knew some people. They told me, "You are making a fool of yourself. This storm will last a week or more."

That wind sure was howling. It went around the house like a spy, testing doors and windows.

The next morning the storm had died down. Nothing stirred. It was as if the earth had come to a standstill. The sun came up. It was big and red and glowing so brightly I had to close my eyes. The snow turned bright red, reflecting the sun. It sparkled, millions and millions of crystals glistening. When I started walking, the snow made a sound like breaking eggshells. That was the only sound I could hear.

When I arrived at Mrs. Elk Head's log house she was sitting in the middle of the room, waiting for me. There was a fragrance in the place, smoke from burning sweetgrass and cedar.

I noticed a big canvas bundle,
about the size of a man. The old
lady asked me to unwrap it. The
bundle consisted of seven raw-
hides, buffalo skin, deer skin,
red and blue flannel. I came to
the last layer and there was the
pipe--Ptehincala Huhu Canun-
pa--the Buffalo Calf Pipe, the
most sacred thing in the world
for me.

Mrs. Elk Head said, "Takoja,
Grandson. Always pass the pipe
to your left. Always take it with
the right. Give it from
your heart, keep the head close
to your heart. Let the spirit
come to you."

I held the pipe. The bowl was my
flesh. The stem stood for all the
generations. I felt my blood
going into the pipe, I felt it coming back, I felt it circling in my
mind like some spirit. I felt the
pipe come alive in my hands, I
felt it move. I felt a power sur-
ging into my body, filling all of
me. Tears were streaming down
my face. And in my mind I got a
glimpse of what that pipe
meant.

That Buffalo Calf pipe made me
know myself, made me know the
earth around me. Healed the
blindness of my heart and made
me see another world beyond
the everyday world of the green
frog skin.

I saw that the pipe was my
church, a little piece of stone
and wood, but I would need nothing more as long as I had this.
I knew that within this pipe
were all the powers of nature,
that within this pipe was me. I
knew that when I smoked the
pipe I was at the center of all
things, giving myself to the
Great Spirit, and that I also re-
leased something of myself that
wanted to be free and that thereby I gladdened all the plants
and animals on earth.

All this I could understand only
with my heart and blood. Even
now, after so much time has
passed since that moment, the
memory of it keeps me awake at
night.

We Indians hold the pipe of
peace. With the pipe, which is
part of us, we shall be praying
for peace. We must try to use
the pipe for mankind. We must
try to get back on the red road
of the pipe, the road of life.

This can be done only if all of
us, Indians and non-Indians
alike, can again see ourselves as
part of the earth.

Being a living part of the earth,
we cannot harm any part of her
without hurting ourselves.

Maybe through this sacred pipe
we can teach each other again
to see through that cloud of pol-

lution which politicians, indus-
trialists and technical experts
hold up to us as "reality."
Through this pipe maybe we can
make peace with our greatest
enemy who dwells deep within
ourselves.

When an Indian prays he
doesn't read a lot of words out of
a book. He just says a very short
prayer.

If you say a long one you don't
understand yourself what you
are saying.

And so the last thing I can teach
you, if you want to be taught by
an old man living in a dilapida-
ted shack, a man who went to
the third grade for eight years, is
this prayer, which I use when I
am crying for a vision:

"Wakan Tanka, Tunkashila, on-
shimala...Grandfather Spirit,
pity me, so that my people may
live."

Curtain falls.

SITTING BULL

A Play in Two Acts

NOTES

When Sitting Bull had a sympathetic, gifted interpreter his
words reveal an agile, clever, profound and thoughtful mind.
The play attempts to reproduce his language without resorting
to interpretation or translation.

All pictographs shown, with the exception of Amos Bad Heart Bull's
rendition of the battle against Custer, were drawn by Sitting Bull himself.

They are reproduced from engravings made for Harper's Weekly,
supplement of July 29, 1876, pp. 625-628.

CAST

TATANKA INYOTAKE, called Sitting Bull, a chief of the Lakota
    Sioux.

JAMES MCLAUGHLIN, US government Indian agent.

MRS. MCLAUGHLIN, his wife.

CATHERINE WELDON, missionary, Sitting Bull's friend.

WILLAM F. "BUFFALO BILL" CODY, showman, ex-buffalo hunter.

BULLHEAD, Sioux warrior, later policeman at Standing Rock
    Indian reservation.

LT. COL. GEORGE A. CUSTER, US Cavalry officer.

JEB, a luckless prospector.

VERMILYE, railroad agent.

JAMES WALSH, officer of the royal Canadian Mounted Police.

CROW FOOT, Sitting Bull's son.

SHAVE HEAD & RED TOMAHAWK, policemen at Standing Rock.

A BOY and his FATHER.

A US soldier.

ACT I

Curtain rises on a sideshow in
William F. "Buffalo Bill" Cody's Wild
West Show. At center stage on a
slightly elevated platform sits a
proud, imperious Lakota Sioux chief
and medicine man: SITTING BULL. He
wears ceremonial headdress, clothes
and beads and has in back and around
him what a 19th century showman would
consider typical Indian artifacts:
tomahawk, drum, a buckskin over
buffalo hide shield on which is
painted a huge bird, a long lance
adorned with dried scalps. All these
rest in front of an authentic
recreation of a Sioux tepee. Behind
all this is a wall tapestried with a

large red white and blue American
flag; it contains 46 stars. Enter a
group of men and women, among them
CATHERINE WELDON and a small boy and
his father. They stare at Sitting
Bull, murmur and whisper excitedly
among themselves.
A middle-aged woman of mixed blood,
MRS. JAMES MCLAUGHLIN, stands
somewhat apart.

FATHER
Is it really him?

MRS. MCLAUGHLIN
Yes indeed, that's him.

CATHERINE
(awed)
Sitting Bull.

MRS. MCLAUGHLIN
If you want do say something to him, go ahead. I will
interpret for you.

CATHERINE
He doesn't understand any English?

MRS. MCLAUGHLIN
Nothing that he will admit to. He is a very stubborn
character.

FATHER
And dangerous. Don't get too close, son.

BOY
Look at that lance, Pa. It could tear your guts out.

No one shows the temerity to approach
Sitting Bull who rests imperturbable.
BUFFALO BILL CODY enters behind them,
regards the group. He wears a
prominent six-shooter but is
otherwise in mufti prior to his
performance. His long hair is hidden
under a hat.

FATHER

Son, you're looking at the most feared Indian in America.
Killed more white men than you can count. And liked it.

CATHERINE

Did he really kill Custer?

BUFFALO BILL

That's what they say, m'am. With that tomahawk right
there.(more murmuring)

BOY

There's still blood on it, Pa!

BUFFALO BILL

Formidable weapon, isn't it? Some say the bloodthirsty
devil cut out Custer's heart, took it in his hands just
like a cob of corn and ate it. (a little gasp of horror
from Catherine; Cody steps forward.) No need to be
frightened, folks. We've tamed him right good. Long as I've
got this (patting holster) he'll do you no harm. Go on. If
you ask him real polite and give him a dollar, he might
even give you his autograph. Would you like that, son?

BOY

You bet!

FATHER

That's not cheap but shoot, that's the most famous Indian
in America
          (forks over the silver to his son)

BUFFALO BILL

Go on, son.

                    The boy edges forward, followed
                    behind by his nervous father. Without
                    changing expression, Sitting Bull
                    takes paper and quill which just
                    happen to be at his side, begins to
                    trace on the page.

CATHERINE

Look at him. I expected a wild beast, but he's almost
handsome. In a primitive sort of way. Has he accepted the
Lord?

BUFFALO BILL
M'am, to him our God is just another white man.

CATHERINE
Does he really hate us so much?

BUFFALO BILL
His blood fairly boiled with rage. He wanted to kill us
all. But he's realized you can't stop Manifest Destiny.

CATHERINE
They say he's had four wives.

BUFFALO BILL
Yes m'am. He comes by his name naturally.

CATHERINE
Goodness.

BUFFALO BILL
He could be the richest man on the reservation. Buy himself
a real house and move out of that shack he calls home. But
every buck he earns ends up in the pockets of street
urchins and vagabonds.

CATHERINE
It's plain he doesn't know the value of a dollar.

> In b.g. the son has given his father
> the paper over which he puzzles as
> Sitting Bull slips the silver dollar
> in the boy's pocket, to his surprise
> and amusement. A small smile plays
> over Sitting Bull's face.

FATHER
Hey, what's this? Tunky...tanky...

> He hands the page to Mrs. McLaughlin
> who looks at what Sitting Bull has
> written.

MRS. MCLAUGHLIN
He wrote his name in Sioux.

FATHER
Injun language!

BOY

It's all right, Pa.

MRS. MCLAUGHLIN

Here, I'll translate it for you. (scribbles) See, "Sitting Bull."

>   The father still looks dubious, less
>   than pleased. A valet enters. He has
>   in his arms a brilliant gold buckskin
>   vest, huge white Stetson. Cody doffs
>   his hat, takes the Stetson. His long
>   blond locks tumble down.

BOY

Hey, you're Buffalo Bill!

>   The group excitedly surround him,
>   begging autographs from the legendary
>   Indian fighter. In b.g., Sitting Bull
>   is forgotten. Off stage is heard the
>   sound of a band, an opening fanfare.

BUFFALO BILL

Now folks, plenty of time for autographs later. Would you be kind enough to take them to their seats, Mrs. Maclaughlin? Show starts in five minutes.

>   They head off stage, jabbering
>   excitedly.

BOY

Wow, I met Buffalo Bill!

>   Cody and Sitting Bull are left alone.

BUFFALO BILL

Dammit Bull, you want to go back to farming taters on the reservation? It's called North Dakota now. Not big Sioux hunting ground. You're living in a white man's world. Haven't I been good to you? Showed you Chicago, New York, Washington? You met the President of the United States, the Great White Father. Write your white name! It's "Sitting Bull." Sitting Bull.

> He puts on the Stetson, heads off
> stage. In a moment we hear the roar
> of the crowd's greeting. Sitting Bull
> remains silent for a moment, then
> stands, turns to the audience.

SITTING BULL

My name is Tatanka Inyotake. At one time I was chief of all
the Lakota Sioux nations. This honor had never before been
given.

> He moves forward to address the
> audience. He will move around the
> stage as the spirit moves him.

SITTING BULL

When I was a boy the Sioux owned the world: the sun rose
and set on our land; we sent thousands of men into battle.
What they now call North Dakota was only part of the land
we loved--where we lived, moving from place to place as the
sun moved in the sky. If you know this earth, you will
learn very much about me and my people. Much of it is
plains. You can ride and ride and ride and see nothing in
the distance. And when you do see something, a small rise
maybe, and think, soon I'll reach it and be able to see an
end to this endless journey, you realize that soon means
later, so much the distance fools your eyes. You are alone,
and if you are not strong of heart, the loneliness will
panic you. I have seen men, white men, go mad. You say to
yourself, if only the clouds would come. Thunder. A break
in the big sky that stretches forever. You'll say wrong.

Here the storms beat the earth with a violence I can't
describe. You have to come and feel what it's like
yourself. And then you'll say, I won't come again. It's for
this reason so many suns and moons passed and no one
roamed this land but the Sioux. We were great warriors, strong
because we had to be. I was born in the year of the great
snowfall. We do not measure time with numbers, what you
call dates. Because this was never understood, many people
died. (shakes his head sadly)
My father was the first Tatanka Inyotake. He was a chief.
He owned a great many ponies in four colors, so he was very
rich. My mother was a good woman. She loved to laugh and
make people laugh. In the beginning I was called Jumping
Badger, but no one called me that. I took my time to
decide. I reflected. So they called me "Slow." This was not

a flattering name for someone who was to become the fastest runner in the tribe, but it was better than Jumping Badger.

I was only 10 when I killed my first buffalo. Even so young, I had such skill riding with bow and arrow. It is not an easy thing at full gallop, among a thousand buffalo raising thunder with their hooves, to load and shoot an arrow. Already I was famous as a hunter. Yet I gave the calves that I killed to the poor that had no horses. I was considered a good man.

        Lights up on BULLHEAD, a fierce
        looking warrior in full battle dress.

        BULLHEAD
Once he shot his arrow first and killed a wild partridge I had been hunting too. When he saw the sadness on my face he gave me the bird and went hungry that night and the next night. He was that generous.

        SITTING BULL
After that Bullhead would follow me anywhere.

BULLHEAD

Wherever he was and whatever he did his name was great everywhere. He knew how to choose the best and fastest horses and he always led the charge. He would ride without saddle or bridle, gripping his horse's mane, naked except for his lance and shield, lunging from side to side so his enemies could hardly see him.

SITTING BULL

We made war, but you have to understand, it was as natural to us as ice cracking in rivers when the spring sun came. A young man feeling his full strength for the first time, he had to show his bravery. Maybe a Crow warrior crossed into our territory. Maybe they cut out some bulls from the buffalo herd we were tracking. Maybe we didn't need any reason. Youth doesn't. Riding out to meet another warrior, that was courage.

BULLHEAD

We'd ride behind yelling, "Tatanka Inyotake tahoksila! We are Sitting Bull's boys! We are Sitting Bull's boys!" Sometimes they'd scatter like windblown dust, so much did his very name bring fear. So much did he give us courage.

SITTING BULL

It was more important to count coup than to kill. Riding straight toward an Assiniboine or Blackfoot or Crow with his rifle or bow and arrow trained toward your heart, riding into his face at full gallop, stretching out your lance...and touching him with the blade, just a touch...that was counting coup. What could be more brave than that? We didn't have to kill. Of course, if the warrior you touched couldn't live with the shame to his pride and came after you, then you would do what your own pride demanded. Better to give up your scalp than honor.

> He is silent for a moment. Then
> fingers the scalps.

SITTING BULL

These are not from children or women. For us, there was no honor unless your enemy saw you coming. Your measured your fear against his, and the one blessed with greater strength that day lived.

BULLHEAD

The morning of a great fight he would shout, "It's a good day to die!"

SITTING BULL

If you are ready to die, you are ready to fight. For your home, family, honor and pride.

Lights down on Bullhead.

There was room for everybody to show his honor. Then when it was done, to return home. Everyone respected homes. No one would never attack during sleep, a feast, or dancing the Sun Dance.

I was also a spiritual man. I did not cure our people in the way you think, like a medicine man, but I had visions. I could see sometimes into the future, whether the buffalo would come again in the spring, when or where our enemies might attack. Very often the birds spoke to me in songs I could understand.

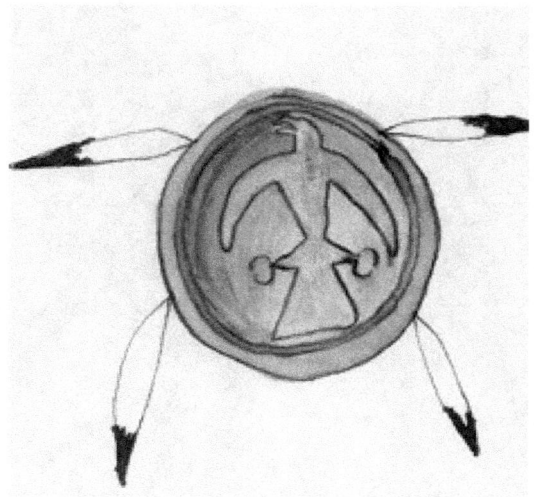

Sitting Bull's Shield

(Sitting Bull takes his lance from beside the tepee.) We spent much of our lives following the buffalo, hunting to feed our people. Fighting our enemies. In winter snow on the Plains can fall for weeks, with a wind that freezes through all the buffalo robes you can wear. Together in our tipi homes around the warm fire, we talked, played, made love, enjoyed our children. We told them stories, the legends of our people. Where we came from, how the world came to be, how the White Buffalo Woman brought us the pipe of peace and sharing between all earth's creatures. We sang songs.

He pauses a moment, remembering.

SITTING BULL

Then the white people came. Like a flood that had no end.
They were like no enemy we ever faced. When we killed the
buffalo, we thanked him for giving his flesh to keep us
alive. What kind of people would kill a whole race of animals
for sport? What drove them? Fear? Greed? Madness? We were
accustomed to warfare, but we never wanted to conquer. We
did not understand. They laughed when we tried to speak
their language. We would have laughed when they tried to
speak ours, but they never tried. We were primitive savages.
Our tongue was not worth learning, except by a few trappers
and traders who had to learn it. If they couldn't understand
our language, it wasn't worth understanding. They were like
blades of grass on the prairie. Once they took root, nothing
could remove them. Not fire, storms, the awful winds that
blow in winter...or us. They came with knives and guns and
hatred. They hoped we would fight. They wanted us to fight.

> Stage brightens to reveal LT. COLONEL
> GEORGE A. CUSTER seated at his desk
> trying to placate a prospector, JED,
> who paces impatiently. His long blond
> locks dangling to his shoulders
> resemble Buffalo Bill's. Sitting Bull
> watches the colloquy.

CUSTER

I'd advise you not to go into the Black Hills till my Army
arrives.

JED

Col. Custer, the first one there gets the most. That's what
they say. That's what I believe.

CUSTER

Yes but you see, the Hills aren't officially open to
prospecting yet. We're trying to break the news gently to
the Sioux.

JED

You know what I say? The hell with them. Bunch of heathens
taking up space. Preacher wants to give 'em the gospel, I
say fine. We'll send 'em to Hell that much
quicker.

CUSTER
They're a stubborn lot of savages and they put up a
fearsome front, but in my experience, one charge from me
and my bluecoats and they turn tail like prairie chickens.
In six months I'll have them rounded up and tamed and you
can settle down in peace.

JED
Don't you fret, Colonel. Long as I've got this (patting his
rifle) they're the ones to be worrying. They start to aim
one of them little arrows, I'll just pop an eye out, bang!
I'm gonna get me that gold. Every time I bite into a
chicken, you ain't gonna see nuthin' but yeller! My
scrabbling days is done. (he heads off, exiting stage in a
gold rush.)

Lights down on Custer.

SITTING BULL
He was right about that. (fingering one of the scalps on
rack) This man measured me in his sights. He held his
ground, trusting his nerve, waiting to see my eyes flush
before him. I charged so close I could see his hand slowly
tightening the rifle trigger. Slowly, because he trusted
his courage. But I gouged my horse toward him, screaming my
war cry. At the last second, his eyelids twitched. Fear?
Wonder? Doubt? The wind from his bullet scorched my side-
here. Later my brothers praised my courage. Was it that?
Maybe I was just crazy, crazy mad with anger. They say I
hated white men. No. I hated the future they brought. Back
then, we didn't know. We only wanted to go on with our
lives, just like before. We didn't understand. Our eyes
didn't see far enough.

The Earth we call our Mother. She nourishes us, warms us,
is always there. We came from her, and when we die return
to her womb. White men never realized this when they asked
to sell our land. How could we sell our Mother?
We called it our land because it was where we always lived.
Where the spirits of our religion lived. A certain mountain
could be holy. We loved most of all the Black Hills.

> Lights up on JAMES MCLAUGHLIN, in his
> early '40s, short and stocky, with a
> neat imperial and a bowler hat
> covering thick wavy hair.

MCLAUGHLIN
The war which had its culmination in the Custer affair
originated primarily in the need for giving the white man
the privilege of mining in the Black Hills.

SITTING BULL
We loved these hills. Wild game roamed there. Whenever we
were hungry, we could go into these hills and find all the
food we wanted. There were trees and wood for our tipis.
There were Spirits.

MCLAUGHLIN

Other excuses were made. It was said that it was necessary
to get the Indians on reservations in order to permit
travel through the country; that they were hostiles and
engaged in continuous warfare, all of which was true
enough; but this did not deter the government from sending
Lt. Col. Custer on an expedition into the Black Hills in
1874.

SITTING BULL

There was a treaty. I had never signed it. Some chiefs did.
But even this treaty gave us these hills as our home. PAHA
SAPA, "hills that are black."

MCLAUGHLIN

There was no doubt about the language of the treaty. No
attempt was made to get an amendment, and neither is there
any doubt that its provisions were ignored. The Indians
believed themselves to be absolute owners of the land, and
their right to it was undisputed, subject to the right of
eminent domain in the United States

SITTING BULL

After Longhair Custer led his soldiers there, more and more
whites came in.

MCLAUGHLIN

As there must have been in view of the official statement
that the country was rich in gold.

SITTING BULL

We resisted. We fought. The whites then claimed we were
enemies who could not be reasoned with.

MCLAUGHLIN

The white man would not stay out and the Indian must be
gotten out. Of course there was no use quarreling with this
condition.

SITTING BULL

They sent us a message: come to the Indian agency by this
date, or it will go very bad for you. What did it signify,
"January"? Their calendars were meaningless to us.
Imagine this: tell a proud independent people to go live in a
cage. Change their whole way of life. Why? Because they said
so. Imagine this: In less than 2 moons, move tribes, all men

and women and children through the snow and cold of a
Dakota winter. Have you ever tried to cross an ice-swollen river
in the dead of winter? On foot, with your women and children,
some with month-old babies? We didn't understand. Who
could? We stayed in camp. The winter passed slowly. It was
almost the time for flowers but that year the flowers came late,
so fierce was the cold. So our brother Minneconjous and their
friends the Cheyenne were sleeping that terrible dawn on the
Power River, warm as they could be in the many tepees spread
out peacefully along the bank.

The white soldiers attacked without warning, shooting and
riding down men, women and children in the defenseless gray
of dawn. Without warning. Or mercy. Or regret. I saw dead
babies, their heads crushed into the mud by their horses'
hooves. (pause) Longhair Custer called us "barbaric."
Those who lived came to me and Crazy Horse, struggling
through the frozen snow. Now we understood.
I invited all the tribes to come join us, Oglala Sioux led by
Crazy Horse, Gall, Red Cloud, all the great warrior chiefs.
Even some of our enemies. I told them, come together, let
them see how united we are, how we want to keep our land
and our life. Many many came.

It was the largest gathering of tribes any of us had ever
seen. We felt strong, confident that the white army would
leave us alone.

We camped on the creek we called Greasy Grass. We talked,
spoke of what to do. Many felt, if we were going to see the
end, it was good to see it together, go to the spirit world
together.

They had sent the Army, 3 whole divisions, one led by
Longhair Custer. Much later I learned they had the idea to

surround us with an overwhelming force of soldiers with their
rifles and guns and good medicine of the Great White Father.
They were convinced we would never listen, never make peace.
So why would anyone talk with us?

Not Longhair Custer. He was impatient. He wanted to get there
first, hog all the fame. Longhair drove his men without stop.
The night before I went up to the hilltop that spread over
all the plains to the east, where our troubles always came. I
cut my flesh into so many pieces I could not count. I prayed.
"Wakan Tanka, pity me. I offer you this pipe in the name of
the tribe. Wherever are the sun, moon, earth and four points
of the wind, there always you are. Father, save the tribe.
Pity me. We want to live. Guard us against all misfortunes or
calamities. Pity me."

Then I had my vision...white soldiers falling like rain. I
descended into our camp, bleeding all over from my sacrifice.
I told the chiefs, the white soldiers will come to kill us,
and they will attack, but if we keep strong together, victory
will be ours.

They did come.
When they rode on the bluffs, Longhair could not wait.
Down below he saw nothing but glory. It blinded him.
Longhair, the greatest white man in the land, victor over
Crazy Horse and Gall and Sitting Bull.

First Longhair sent a company onto the plain. Many of our
me were by the river, swimming with their wives and children.
The soldiers came charging, shooting at every Indian in
sight, women and children too. They killed the family of
Chief Gall, his wife and two children, defenseless innocents.
And others.
But the warrior men rallied quickly and rode to the defense.
Their hearts were storming with rage. They remembered the
words I had spoken the night before. We stopped the soldiers'
charge, then drove them back. They panicked, fled to a
bivouac...all that was left of that hard-riding band now
cowered behind whatever shelter they could find. We would
have wiped them out, but by then Longhair had come.

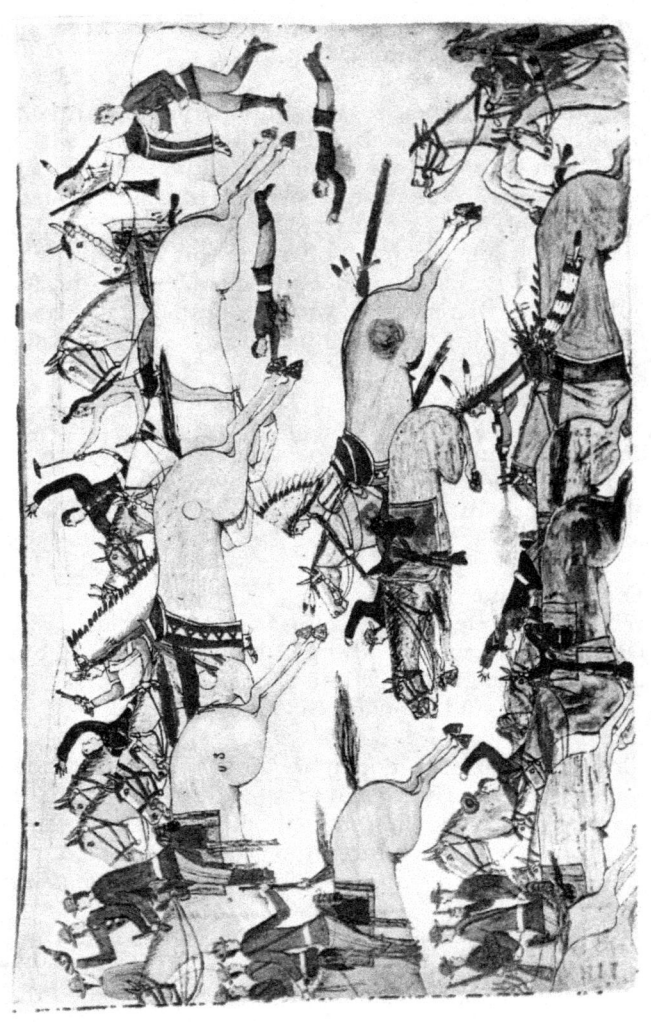

His plan was to descend a coulee to the river and while we were occupied with the other soldiers, attack us in the rear, Longhair leading as always, sure of his invincibility, trumpets blaring, his men shouting as if the sound of their voices alone would make us tremble before greater men.

No. We fought. A few, their bravery we would sing for a generation, held Longhair at the river until the mass of warriors left off the siege. This great force drove Longhair back, up the ridge to its crest.
There they formed a defense...such as it was. White people called this a last stand and sang the bravery of the bluecoats. Do you want to know the truth? These men broke ranks at first opportunity.

> As he voice rises toward his
> peroration the sounds of battle
> become louder: gunfire, horses
> whinnying, Indians yelling war cries,
> and and voices of panicked men
> pleading for mercy by screaming over
> and over the name "John!"

SITTING BULL
Some fled toward a ravine, running like scared rabbits. We wiped them out there. The dust rose so thick it was hard to see, but we could see the men who d come to kill us and our hearts were bad. Gall swung his club and killed and killed, so strong was his anger and desolation. Did we know Custer was there, did we know who killed him? No. All we knew was that these people had come to kill us, our women and children.

> His voice rises in rage until at the
> end he is almost shouting.

SITTING BULL
They thought we would run. They thought we were nothing, savages who had no love for their people and homes and had no right to live. We showed them then what we were, proud warriors who would fight for all the Great Spirit can give men to fight for. Crazy Horse gathered the Sioux and Cheyenne and led a charge right toward those who were left.

Many yelled in fear, begging for the mercy they would never have given to us. They kept crying "John! John!" as if we had no names of our own. We rode them down. Didn't they know we were men? Didn't they know we had names? I have a name and I am a man! I am Tatanka Inyotake!

>He raises his right arm with lance in hand and shakes it toward the high heaven, screaming his war cry "Aiyyyeee!" The cry resounds.

>Lights down.

ACT TWO

SCENE 1

While stage is still dark, a
melancholy song sung by Sitting Bull
reverberates throughout theater:

SONG (OFF)
I - ki - ci - ze wa-on kon he wa - na he - na - la ye - lo
he i - yo - ti - ye ki - ya wa-on.("A warrior I have been.
Now it is all over. A hard time I have."

After a few moments the song ends.
Lights up on Sitting Bull
standing before a tepee but all has
changed. The tepee is ragged and
weatherworn. Sitting Bull's robes and
raiment reflect acute poverty. A
dirty shirt, torn leggings, a ragged
blanket around his waist, a
handkerchief drawn around his head.
The rest of his family huddling
together for warmth behind him are
just as poorly clothed in rotting
garments.
We can hear the winter wind howling.

SITTING BULL
(to audience)
I sing this song very often now. There are only a few
words. In your language, "A warrior I have been, now it is
all over. A sad time I have. » (he looks somber, distant)

A uniformed Royal Canadian Mounted
policeman, JAMES WALSH, enters
stage. There is a slight pause as
Walsh waits for Sitting Bull to leave
the world of spirit song and returns
to a hard reality. Sitting Bull
notices his presence.

SITTING BULL
My son, you have come to speak the truth. Now speak it if
your heart wishes.

WALSH

It is a hard truth. I don't want to say it but you asked
to. If you hadn't I would have left you free and proud as
you are, except...

SITTING BULL

Except my people are starving. No man can be a fool and
live as before when the children cry all night and the
women have nothing more in their bellies and breasts to
give.

WALSH

We are under so much pressure from the United States
government for giving you refuge. It's been two years now
but even so, well, I'm afraid you will never live down your
victory over Custer and the United States Army.

SITTING BULL

You've been a good friend, like all the redcoats. You have
won my respect. Your land, will always be honored when men
look back and say, the Sioux were welcome here.

WALSH

I wish I could have done more.

Bullhead storms across stage.

BULLHEAD

I will not surrender! We have not been beaten in battle.
Tatanka Inyotake, let us go again to the land of Blackfeet
or Crows and count coup.
I will follow you wherever you want, and if any white man
dares to challenge us, we will kill him!

SITTING BULL

Bullhead, I know the sorrow in your heart. But the
Blackfeet ride no more. They, the Crows, the Cheyenne,
Kiowas and Commanche, all these great tribes live in peace
with the white man.

BULLHEAD

Like sheep in a corral!

SITTING BULL

Like sheep. But they live.

BULLHEAD
In dishonor and shame.

SITTING BULL
Listen to me, my brother. When our enemy could not vanquish
us, they killed the buffalo. Now we have nothing to eat. We
are starving. A brave warrior sees when the battle is won
or lost and lays down his weapon. A man can be beaten and
still keep his pride.

BULLHEAD
Never!

   Bullhead gestures in defiance, then
   strides off and exits.

SITTING BULL
In his heart he is proud and lives to be the man he always
was. If I were not a chief...

WALSH
Are you ready to meet the Americans?

SITTING BULL
As ready as they are.

   Walsh exits. Sitting Bull turns as
   his son CROW FOOT approaches.

CROW FOOT
What will they do to us, Father?

SITTING BULL
Me they may put in what they call a prison. The worst thing
a free man can endure, a small cage where no sun passes.
You and your mother and all our people, for you they have
chosen the worst land to live on, land no one wants but a
few vegetables, and if they could speak, even they would
look elsewhere.

CROW FOOT
Tell me you will not let them kill you.

SITTING BULL
My son, know this--I will never bow to the bluecoats.

   He hands the boy his rifle.

SITTING BULL
Come. We will go back as we left, in pride and honor.

They exit stage.

SCENE 2

A salon, decked out with some Indian
paraphernalia as if to give comfort to
the guest of honor. ENTER a group of
people including MACLAUGHLIN, his half
Sioux wife MRS. MCLAUGHLIN, VERMILYE,
BUFFALO BILL, CATHERINE WELDON and a
uniformed U.S. SOLDIER.

VERMILYE
And here he is, ladies and gentlemen, the great chief
Sitting Bull.

Sitting Bull enters. He is now dressed
in his ceremonial robe. No one of them
seems to know how to react or what to
say, so Sitting Bull takes the lead.
Crow Foot comes behind, carrying a
rifle.

SITTING BULL
I wish it to be remembered that I was the last man of my
tribe to surrender my rifle. I surrender this rifle to you
through my young son, Crow Foot. I wish him to learn the
habits of the whites and to be educated as their sons are
educated. This boy has given it to you, and he now wants to
know how to earn his living.

Crow Foot hands the rifle to the
soldier. There is APPLAUSE from the
group.

MCLAUGHLIN
This is my wife, Mrs. Mclaughlin. Your interpreter.

MRS. MCLAUGHLIN
My husband is the government agent. You must listen to him.
He wants to help you with your new life.

SITTING BULL
You speak English very well.

MRS. MCLAUGHLIN
He helped teach me. If you cannot make yourself understood,
I will translate for you.

SITTING BULL
You have a hard job. White men have never understood me.

VERMILYE
Chief, I have been authorized by the company I represent,
the Northern Pacific Railroad, to invite you as our guest
to a reception. A lot has happened in the last four years
and I can say proudly that this progress arrived on our
railway. (some applause from the assembled.) You saw the
train outside, Chief. What do you think?

SITTING BULL
It goes fast. Is that what you call progress?
         (After a beat...)

VERMILYE
Well yes, I guess we do! (general laughter)

                    Vermilye holds out his hand to shake.
                    Sitting Bull just stares at it, not
                    knowing what to do.

MRS. MCLAUGHLIN
You must take his hand and shake it. Like this.

                    She hastily seizes his hand and
                    shakes it vigorously.

SITTING BULL
Why? We are not pumping water.

MRS. MCLAUGHLIN
Please do this!

SITTING BULL
For such a beautiful woman, I will not say no.

                    He grabs Vermilye's hand and shakes it
                    like a water pump. After some moments

of this Mrs. Mclaughlin has to grab his
arm and wrench it free of Vermilye's.

SITTING BULL
This is the most ridiculous thing I have ever done.

MCLAUGHLIN, starched up even more
than ordinary by a suit pressed rock
hard and a bowler hat that raises his
height, has been watching impatiently
all these interactions with Sitting Bull.
Now he steps forward.

MCLAUGHLIN
It is perfectly normal. White men do this when we meet new
people or agree on something. This is part of the culture
you will have to learn.

MRS. MCLAUGHLIN
My husband is the agent at Standing Rock reservation, where
you are going to live.

Sitting Bull takes his hand and pumps
it vigorously. Once again Mrs.
McLaughlin has to step in, freeing her
husband.

MCLAUGHLIN
You only have to do it the first time you meet. After, it's
not necessary.

SITTING BULL
Uuless we agree on something. Yes?

MCLAUGHLIN
Yes.

Sitting Bull and McLaughlin stare at
each other for a long moment. Neither
can find anything to say. The silence
is broken as Buffalo Bill, dressed in a
buckskin jacket, comes up to Sitting
Bull.

BUFFALO BILL
You probably know who I am.

SITTING BULL
I probably do. But I forgot.

BUFFALO BILL
William F. Cody, but everyone calls me Buffalo Bill. Does that ring a bell? (to his puzzled look) Does my name mean something?

SITTING BULL
Carcasses. Bones and skeletons of dead buffalo all across the prairie.

BUFFALO BILL
Listen, the Army paid me to provide food for their soldiers. I was doing my job.

SITTING BULL
If they paid you by the head, you are, how do you say, a very rich man.

BUFFALO BILL
Enough. Listen, I'm using that money to mount a Show. For people in the East and who knows, maybe other countries too. Let's be honest with each other, Bull. We can't bring back the buffalo, but we can show people how we lived in the Wild West. Cowboys and Indians too. I'd like you to join me. A chief, representing all the tribes, like you were before...before now.

SITTING BULL
Me, Tatanka Inyotake?

BUFFALO BILL
Sitting Bull, the man who killed Custer. Believe me, you'll open people's eyes.

SITTING BULL
A blind man's eyes are wide open, but he sees nothing. I will think on your proposition.

BUFFALO BILL
Toksa akhe.

MCLAUGHLIN
He will be living on the reservation at Standing Rock under my authority. He cannot leave it without my permission.

BUFFALO BILL
Mr. McLaughlin, I meant to speak with you, sir. We'll be
needing an interpreter. I was wondering if Mrs.
McLaughlin...she'd have a salary and room and board. In
fact we'd welcome both of you.

MCLAUGHLIN
My duties keep me at home. As for her, what about it my
dear, would you like to see the world for a little while?
(she nods emphatically; then McLaughlin to Buffalo Bill)
Just between you and me, she can keep an eye on the old
reprobate.

A young JOURNALIST approaches Sitting
Bull.

JOURNALIST
Mr. Bull, I wonder if I might ask you a few questions. I am
a journalist for, well several newspapers.

SITTING BULL
You look like a brave young man.

JOURNALIST
Thank you.

SITTING BULL
Have you killed many men in battle?

JOURNALIST
No. This is my weapon.
        (brandishing pen)
Right now I want to use it for you.

SITTING BULL
It might kill a mouse but they are bad eating.

JOURNALIST
No, you see I will use it to record whatever you say and it
will be read, that is go to many people, many white people.
This is the moment when you can speak the truth without any
fear.

SITTING BULL
I have always done that. This you can record.

JOURNALIST

Well then, I would like to ask you about Col. Custer.

SITTING BULL

We called him Longhair, because he had long hair. Did you know he had a child by an Indian woman?

JOURNALIST

Why no, I didn't. This is very very surprising--

SITTING BULL

You told me to speak the truth.

JOURNALIST

To my knowledge, he never recognized any such child.

SITTING BULL

Yes, that would have been very surprising.

JOURNALIST

Er, chiefs like Gall and Red Cloud have said that Col. Custer was the last man to fall and fought bravely to the end, quote--that means these are their exact words--"we never saw a braver man." Of course, they said this just after their surrender. Do you think they were being sincere in their assessment of Col. Custer?

SITTING BULL

My son, you know very well, Indians would never be so clever as to tell the white man what he wanted to hear.

JOURNALIST

Well uh, now, some have said that after his death, you cut out his heart and ate it--is this true?

SITTING BULL

You have to understand, there was a bullet in it.

The journalist nods, a bit shocked.

SITTING BULL

Many of my people after the raid on Washita said he had no heart, but you see, they were wrong. Unfortunately, he could not see the nose on his face. He was a fool who rode to his death.

VERMILYE

Well Chief, I've got to turn you over to the authorities
now. Good luck to you. Er, do you know the expression "good
luck?"

SITTING BULL

Yes. The meadowlark sang to me and said I left mine in the
land of the redcoats.

VERMILYE

Well uh,I hope you liked our little party.

SITTING BULL

If this is surrender, it's not so bad.

They all exit, McLaughlin trailing
behind Sitting Bull.

SCENE 3

Lights up on Sitting Bull with
Catherine Weldon. She is dressed like a
schoolmarm and carrying a large black
Bible.

CATHERINE

I am Madame Catherine Weldon. Do you remember meeting
me at Buffalo Bill's Wild West Show? (no response)
Well, no matter. You can call me "Catherine." Do you
understand?

SITTING BULL

Yes. You can call me "Sitting."

CATHERINE

Very good. I see you have made progress in our language.

SITTING BULL

I must. Otherwise white people will consider me a savage.
Tell me Catherine, when white people cannot speak my
language, why can I not consider them savage?

CATHERINE

Well, the short answer is our language is much more complex.

SITTING BULL

This is true. We do not have a word in our tongue for "lie."
We know what it is now, but we never learned this practice.

CATHERINE

I can see your talent for sophistry remains.
Sophistry means to make an argument that
sounds correct but is actually false.

SITTING BULL

Ah, like all the treaties made with us. Now I know why they
were never respected. We will have to adopt this word. It
explains many things.

CATHERINE

Today I've come to introduce you to the Christian religion.

SITTING BULL

I already have a religion. I am not thirsty, but you feel I
need something to drink.

CATHERINE

No sophistry, please. Now Sitting, first things first. You
must stop pretending that your God speaks to you in the song
of a meadowlark. It does not sing your visions. It's just a
bird chattering because he sees a worm.

SITTING BULL
This man the blackrobes were telling me about...Moses.

CATHERINE
Yes...God's chosen instrument.

SITTING BULL
Your God spoke to him in a burning bush?

CATHERINE
Yes.

SITTING BULL
It must have been a short speech.

CATHERINE
The bush was not burned. It stayed just as before, a
flourishing healthy bush. You see, it was a miracle.

SITTING BULL
Your God must be very powerful.

CATHERINE
He knows everything and can do anything.

SITTING BULL
Then why can He not speak to me in the song of a
 meadowlark?

CATHERINE
Because....it is something our God would not do. He would not
use a bird to communicate. Can't you understand that?

SITTING BULL
Yes. Your God would not go (imitating birdsong) "cheep cheep
cheep."

She throws up her hands in
exasperation.

SITTING BULL
Sister--

CATHERINE
I am not your sister! You must stop calling me that.

SITTING BULL
You see, we don't own many things: our lance, shield, horses.
Blankets and headdress we wear for our holy ceremonies.
Eventhese we sometimes share with other members of the
tribe. We call each other "Uncle," "Nephew," even when there's
no blood relation. Our most sacred possessions are our
children. Husbands and wives—

CATHERINE
Yes, wives. I am told you once had two wives living in the
same tepee and God bless you for seeing the light, you
finally just told one to leave.

SITTING BULL
They were always fighting and quarreling.

CATHERINE
No doubt. It's called jealousy. And now?

SITTING BULL
Red Woman stayed and we had a son, Crow Foot, but
then, on a day when grief stormed my heart, she passed to the
spirit world.

CATHERINE
Well, my condolences. Sincere. So who are these two women
living in your tepee now?

SITTING BULL
After I gave some of my best horses for Four Robes--

CATHERINE
Horses? This is how you...procure a wife?

SITTING BULL
A horse is very valuable. And I gave four.

CATHERINE
Not as much as a woman.

SITTING BULL
Yes, of course, that is why we don't trade them for horses.

CATHERINE
My Lord. Well, now you are mongamous, you live with just one
wife?

SITTING BULL
Her sister said she would like to live with us and asked if
she could marry me. We live very well together. They are not
jealous.

CATHERINE
This is called bigamy and it will not do. If you are to
become a good Christian you can have only one wife.

SITTING BULL
Which one should I send away?

CATHERINE
I would think obviously, the one you care for the less.

SITTING BULL
I care for them both. It is against my heart to treat them
differently.

CATHERINE
That is not possible. One you surely must love more than the
other.

SITTING BULL
It depends on the day.

CATHERINE
Oh my Lord. Well then we will have to use order of place.
The second wife should be sent away. Don't worry, she will be
taken care of.

SITTING BULL
I can send them both away--

CATHERINE
Now don't go overboard.

SITTING BULL
—if you will find me a white wife. I am told you just have to
tell them many times "I love you."

CATHERINE
And give a ring. Preferably a diamond ring.

SITTING BULL
It is sad. They are not even worth a horse.

She throws up her hands in despair.

Lights down.

SCENE 4

Sitting Bull and Buffalo Bill enter
stage.

BUFFALO BILL
It's my best show horse, danced two years with Annie Oakley
firing those six-shooters like you wouldn't believe.

SITTING BULL
I will miss Little Sure Shot. If Custer had gone to war
with her he would not be eating grass now.

BUFFALO BILL
I appreciate what you've done for me, Bull. Gonna miss you.

> McLaughlin and his wife enter. She is
> wearing a very broad-brimmed hat with
> flower motifs that covers half her
> face and swoops to the side. The
> effect is less elegant than wished.

MCLAUGHLIN
Delighted to see you again, Mr. Cody. I hope you will give
me and Mrs. Mclaughlin the pleasure of your company at our
evening meal. She's prepared a feast.

BUFFALO BILL
My sincere apologies to you Marie Louise, but I have to be
on my way. We're crossing the Atlantic next week--the
European tour can't wait!

MCLAUGHLIN
So soon? Well, it's a good thing we've bought your
wardrobe. This hat will look good in front of that what do
you call it, Eiffel Tower, don't you think?

> Sitting Bull and Cody exchange
> glances.

SITTING BULL
I will not go.

BUFFALO BILL
That being the case, we won't be needing Mrs. McLaughlin's
services.

MCLAUGHLIN
(to Sitting Bull)
Why the devil not? Since your return you've been even more
inflated with your desire for public attention.

SITTING BULL
I went because I wanted to see the white man's world and
tell how it is to my people. I have done it.

> Mrs. McLaughlin has beeen fighting back
> tears since Sitting Bull's declaration.
> Now she abruptly turns and rushes off
> stage.

BUFFALO BILL
You could take the missus yourself to Paris. Why Mr.
Mclaughlin, that would be the trip of a lifetime. It goes
without saying that if we're there, you're invited as my
special guests.

MCLAUGHLIN
Thank you, but Mr. Cody you can hardly imagine how many
preoccupations I have keeping these recent hostiles on the
path toward righteous living. If I left for even a week, who
knows...

BUFFALO BILL
I do understand sir, and this nation is grateful for your
dedication. Please extend my regrets to Marie Louise.

SITTING BULL
I have seen nothing that a white man has, houses or railways
or clothing or food, that is as good as the right to move in
the open country, and live in our own fashion. The life of
white men is slavery. They are prisoners in towns and farms.
The life my people want is a life of freedom.

> Cody and MacLaughlin exchange looks.

BUFFALO BILL
     (to Sitting Bull)
Toksa akhe.

> He exits stage.

MCLAUGHLIN
I can see you've learned nothing.

> Mclaughlin looks grim, angry and
> determined. He moves over, picks up a
> shovel that has been leaning against
> the wall.

127

MCLAUGHLIN

Now, the first thing you must grasp is the use of tools.
This is called a shovel. It's used to dig and open up the
ground. After you plant the seeds for your future crop.
With a rake you smooth out the earth. It's important to
make separate rows for each vegetable and to make
them straight. I've had a lot of trouble with your tribe
making them understand the concept of a straight line.

SITTING BULL

What is a straight line?

MACLAUGHLIN

Enough said. It goes like this.
        (drawing it)

SITTING BULL

Why is this so important?

MCLAUGHLIN

Many reasons. Mainly it's so you don't mistake a potato
from a turnip when you dig them up. It's organization,
order. The same principle that enabled our soldiers to
defeat you and the other tribes.

SITTING BULL

So if I learn how to make a straight line I will learn how
to fight the white army?

MCLAUGHLIN

No, first because no one follows you any more, and second,
by then God willing we'll have converted you to
agriculture. Now, if the word potato is too complicated for
you, just call it a spud.
        (hands him one; Sitting Bull
        eyes it)

SITTING BULL

"Spud."

MCLAUGHLIN

Easy to grow and very good eating. If you prefer to go
hungry and wait until the buffalo come back, that is your
choice. Here is your shovel, here is your rake. They are
not as sharp as the lance you used to carry, but maybe
they'll do to bring down a big bull. For those on this

reservation who prefer to eat, distribution of rations--and that includes potatoes-- will take place tomorrow, at the Agency. If you are late, you get nothing and will have to wait another month. Now I know you don't measure time as we do, so one full moon. Long time.

He exits stage.

SITTING BULL
So this is my new life. To grow and eat a "spud." I hear of the Ghost Dance. Even if it is a false hope, it is hope.

Lights down.

SCENE 5

Tomtoms and shake-rattles and the rhythmic sing-song chants of Sioux singers echo loudly as Lights up on the Ghost Dance. Several dancers in a circle are swaying to the tom toms and moving slowly in a circle. The beat is ominous, wailing and impressive.

To the side stands Sitting Bull, watching closely and occasionally gesturing at the dancers

McLaughlin and Catherine Weldon enter stage and watch, McLaughlin frowning, Catherine Weldon fascinated by what she witnesses.

As they watch, one of the dancers spins out of the circle and falls at Sitting Bull's feet. The music and dance continue as Sitting Bull leans down and speaks in the ear of the fallen dancer. After a moment, as if revivified and inspired, he gets up and goes back to the dance with new energy and fervor.

After a moment Sitting Bull gestures
to the dancers and they dance off
stage.

MCLAUGHLIN
(to Catherine Weldon)
I succeeded in getting that brutal, completely inhumane Sun
Dance removed from the Sioux's customs. No more tearing the
bloody flesh and hanging suspended in the sun like living
meat. Let me tell you, some people have come to me and
private and thanked me for it--as well they should. And now
like a leopard changing its spots they've started some
nonsense called the Ghost Dance.

CATHERINE
I am sure Sitting Bull has nothing to do with it. I hear it's
a Cheyenne called Kicking Bear.

MCLAUGHLIN
I'm sure he has everything to do with it.

Sitting Bull comes over. He holds out
his hand to shake.

MCLAUGHLIN
We've already met. (Sitting bull lowers hand) Anyway I'm less
interested in your hand than your head and what might be
floating around in it. Everywhere I hear the tom toms and
chants and people falling into hysteria.

CATHERINE
Yes please, tell us honestly, what is this Ghost Dance?

SITTING BULL
I will tell you the story as it was told to me.
Kicking Bear arose after the corn-planting, in his tepee on
the Cheyenne reservation. He traveled far, past the last
signs of white men, for no white man had ever had the courage
to travel so far.

On the evening of the fourth day, weak and faint from his
journey, he looked for a camping-place, and then he saw a
man dressed like an Indian, but whose hair was long and
glistening like the yellow money of the white man. His face
was very beautiful to see, and he said, you have done well.
Leave your horse and follow me.
He led the way up a great ladder of small clouds, and up

130

through an opening in the sky. He took him to the Great
Spirit and his wife, and he saw that they were dressed as
Indians. Then from an opening in the sky he was shown all the
countries of the earth and the camping-grounds of our fathers
since the beginning; all were there, the tepees, the ghosts
of our fathers, great herds of buffalo, and a country that
smiled because it was rich and the white man was not there.
Then the Messiah showed his hands and feet, and there were
wounds in them which had been made by the whites when
they crucified him. And he told him he was going to come
again on earth, and this time he would remain and live with
the Indians, who were his chosen people.

And the Great Spirit spoke saying: -
Take this message to my red children and
tell it to them as I say it. I have neglected the Indians for
many moons, but I will make them my people now if they obey
me in this message. The earth is getting old, and I will make
it new for my chosen people, the Indians, who are to inhabit
it, and among them will be all those of their ancestors who
have died, their fathers, mothers, brothers, cousins and
wives, all those who hear my voice and my words through the
tongues of my children.

Then he was shown the dances and taught the songs that he
brought to us, and he was led down the ladder of clouds.
The Messiah told him to return to our people, and he promised
he would return to the clouds no more, but would remain at
the end of the earth and lead the ghosts of our fathers to
meet us when the next winter is passed.

MCLAUGHLIN
That is the most ridiculous story I have ever heard. Messiah
indeed.
CATHERINE
Sitting Bull, I can assure you that the Great Spirit did not
have a wife.

SITTING BULL
Did he not care for women?

CATHERINE
Alas, this proves you have understood nothing about our
religion.

MCLAUGHLIN

You see how pernicious and foolish this bric-a-brac is?
Look here, Sitting Bull, I want to know what you mean by your
present conduct . Your preaching and practicing of this
absurd Messiah doctrine is causing a great deal of uneasiness
among the Indians on this reservation. You should stop it at
once.

SITTING BULL

I preach it because much good will come to my people.

MCLAUGHLIN

It will bring them all into trouble. You know very well that
it's all rubbish.

SITTING BULL

I will make you a proposition to settle this question. You go
with me to the agencies to the West. Let me seek for the man
who saw the Messiah ; and when we find him, I will demand to
see the Messiah. If he cannot, I will return and tell my
people it is a lie.

MCLAUGHLIN

That would be like trying to catch the wind that blew last
year. Come with me to the agency. I will convince you how
absurd this doctrine is.

SITTING BULL

And if the Messiah comes while I am gone?

CATHERINE

There, you see. Sophistry!

MCLAUGHLIN

I'm afraid that around you his worst instincts surface. Miss
Weldon, as it's clear your lessons have had no effect and the
most scurrilous rumors are circulating about your relation
with this man, I must forbid any further contact. You will
have to leave this reservation.

CATHERINE

What a big strong man you are, sending away a helpless
widow trying to do good.

MCLAUGHLIN

Unfortunately, here we see the result.

CATHERINE
Very well. I will go.

SITTING BULL
(to Catherine)
Remember always the Lakota name I have given you. In your
language, Woman Walks Ahead. If history speaks true, it will
say this.

She exits stage.

SITTING BULL
My heart inclines to do what you request, but I must
consult my people. I will talk to the men to-night, and if
they think it advisable I will go to the agency.

MCLAUGHLIN
At least you are learning the virtues of democracy. Please
do not delay.

He exits stage.
Sitting Bull moves over to a corner of
stage as Lights go down over all but
him.

SITTING BULL
They tell me to believe in the Messiah. But don't believe him
if he says something they do not believe. If he speaks to
Indians. If he promises them happiness, this is the illusion
of an ignorant fool, Kicking Bear. Like their treaties. I must
believe in these treaties that they said they believe in but do
not. And believe in the Messiah because they do. This
sophistry is a wonderful thing.

Lights up on the rest of the stage where
McLaughlin sits at a desk penning a
letter.

MCLAUGHLIN
(voicing aloud what he writes)
I am convinced that this new religion is managed at
Standing Rock by Sitting Bull. He is the high priest and
leading apostle of this latest Indian absurdity.
Having lost his former influence over the Sioux, he plans
to use it to reestablish himself in the leadership of the
people, whom he might then lead in any desperate enterprise
he might direct.

133

SITTING BULL
(to audience)
This agent reminds me of my jealous wives. My people, the
ones who respect me and my word and have not yet sold their
honor to him, even these faithful friends say we could have
a man so much worse. (beat) I trust them. But that does not
help me sleep at nights.

MCLAUGHLIN
Removal of Sitting Bull's malcontents would end all trouble
and uneasiness in the future. With him removed, the
advancement of the Sioux will be more rapid and the interests
of the Government greatly subserved thereby.

As he finishes a man walks in toward
McLaughlin, dressed in the uniform of
an Indian policeman. It is Bullhead.
McLaughlin seals the letter and gives
it to him.

MCLAUGHLIN
Send this out immediately, and get your most trusted men
ready. I have a very important job for you.

BULLHEAD
Yes sir.

He salutes.

MCLAUGHLIN
You are not obliged to salute me, but if it pleases you.

BULLHEAD
Yes sir.

Bullhead exits stage.

SITTING BULL
Things are all mixed up.

Buffalo Bill enters, wobbling on his
feet, thoroughly intoxicated.

BUFFALO BILL
Mr. McLaughlin...letter, Gen'ral Miles (fumbling for it,
reading) I am to sez person Sitting Bull and deliver
said person, Sitting Bull, to nearest com'g of'cer, US.

MCLAUGHLIN
Com'g? Please sir, if I may...(taking letter) have a seat Mr.
Cody, you've obviously come a long way and needed fortifying,
God knows against this cold any means to warm up...(reading)
ah, "Commanding," commanding officer!

BUFFALO BILL
Dammit man, got to stop bloodshed before bloodshed, see? See
what I mean?

MCLAUGHLIN
I echo your sentiments Colonel, 1000 per cent. Please,
(pouring a drink of whiskey) welcome to my humble home.

BUFFALO BILL
If you insist.

MCLAUGHLIN
General Miles should entrust you with more important
missions. I have things well in hand here.

He continues pouring and
Buffalo Bill continues partaking.

MCLAUGHLIN
I hear you're taking your show abroad again, after your
magnificent success, and let me assure you as an amateur but
a man fond of spectacle, here we have outstanding
representatives of the Indian nation in Gall and Red Cloud.
Europe will stand in awe at how we've transformed these once
savage fighters into respectful citizens.

BUFFALO BILL
Europe don't give a damn 'bout respect. Where's Tatanka
Inyotake?

MCLAUGHLIN
Ah, Sitting Bull. I'll take you to him...for the road.
(pouring a hefty drink)

Bull Head

BUFFALO BILL
Killed buffalo. Killed their ways. Let 'em dance, let 'em
sing. Good medicine, peace pipe. Bull, never lied. We lied.

MCLAUGHLIN
Manifest Destiny. Neither he nor we can stop it. The times
are pregnant of great things. On the one hand stands the
white man and he is not standing still. Nothing can deter him
from going forward. If, in the march of civilization, a
people is blotted out, it would not be the first time that
march proved remorseless.

He drones on, calculatedly, and very
soon Cody begins to nods off.

MCLAUGHLIN
It has to be said, many of these are earnestly endeavoring to
adjust themselves to the white man's road. But they are
wavering. Bidden by the leaders of a savage cult to
accept this new doctrine which so strongly appeals to
their traditions and inspirations.

Lights dim on them and rise on Sitting Bull.

SITTING BULL
When I left his show White Hat Bill gave me his best show
horse, or so he said, Little Sure Shot said it was his third
best. Strong, big horse, so I rode him on a hunt. He ran like
the wind, but it was no good. Whenever I had to fire the
sound of the shots made him rear up on his hind legs and
start dancing. Not good for hunting.

He looks over as lights rise and sees
that Buffalo Bill's head has fallen on
the table. He is fast asleep. Bullhead
enters, carrying a letter. McLaughlin
eagerly and quickly takes it, reads.

MCLAUGHLIN
A direct order from the Secretary, empowering me to take
action. General Miles' order means nothing now. Take him to
my bunk. (as Bullhead lifts up the sleeping Buffalo Bill and half
carries him off stage) Lieutenant Bullhead, we have saved to
the world a most royal good fellow and most excellent
showman.

McLaughlin comes forward, delighted
with his stratagem. Both men now
pronounce utterances to audience.

MCLAUGHLIN
The day of the Indian is past.

SITTING BULL
(to Mclaughlin) Our past is yours now. Build your cities
over our bones, but they will not lie quiet. We will always
be there, haunting you for all the broken faith, honor
lost, innocent lives buried in rotten ground.

McLaughlin leaves stage. A corner of
the stage goes dark as Lights go up
on Sitting Bull. After a moment, he
hears the SONG of a MEADOWLARK. He
listens for a moment.

SITTING BULL
We say before a battle, "It is a good day to die." That is
what the meadowlark is singing to me now.
(a beat, listening)
He says, my own people will kill me. (pause)
When I was a boy the Sioux owned the world: the sun rose
and set on our land; we sent thousands of men into battle.
Where are the warriors today? Who slew them? Where are our
lands? Who owns them? What law have I broken? Is it wrong
for me to love my own? Is it wicked for me because my skin
is red? Because I am a Sioux; because I was born where my
father lived; because I would die for my people and my
country?

We hear a persistent knocking. Full
Lights up as Sitting Bull moves across
the stage, then stops as Bullhead
enters, in full police uniform and
armed with a pistol in its holster. He
is backed up by two other Indian
policemen, SHAVE HEAD and RED
TOMAHAWK.

BULLHEAD
We are taking you to the Agency. Do not try to argue.

SITTING BULL
Brother, this is how you treat people, crashing in at dawn
in front of their women and children?

BULLHEAD
You have gone into battle many times before first light.
Now follow me.

SITTING BULL
Do not give orders to your chief.

BULLHEAD
When you bowed down before the white man, I looked up, and
there I saw my chief, taking your rifle. You will come,
now!

> Crow Foot has come on stage from
> behind, a buffalo robe wrapped around
> his shoulders.

CROW FOOT
Your friends have come to help you, Father.

> Off stage we start to hear a rising
> surge of angry voices.

SITTING BULL
(to Bullhead)
Then, in coming so early, you came too late.

BULLHEAD
(getting nervous)
If you resist, there will be a big fight.

SITTING BULL
And you will kill your own people. I see you are ready to
do that, and my heart fills with pity and grief for all of
you. I will come.

> He starts to head out.

CROW FOOT
Father! You call yourself a brave man. You said you would
never surrender to a bluecoat, and now you give yourself up
to Indians in blue coats.

> Sitting Bull stops in his tracks.

SITTING BULL
My son, you honor your people.

> Bullhead nods at Shave Head and Red
> Tomahawk and they grab Sitting Bull's
> arms, try to force him out the door.

SITTING BULL
I am Tatanka Inyotake!

> Sitting Bull with the strength of the
> warrior he has always wrenches his arms
> free with such force that are hurtled

back. Free now, Sitting Bull hurries out the
door of his own will and in a second we
hear his war cry: "Aiyyeeeee!" It is
met by a ROAR from a crowd of friends
waiting. Bullhead and his two
companions pull their guns and run out
after Sitting Bull.

We hear shouts, cries and most of all
gunshots, one after another, at least
thirty of them exploding like thunder.

As they begin to subside Sitting Bull
stumbles onto stage, falls dead. A
moment later as the gunshots cease, a
badly wounded Bullhead lurches onto
stage, falls to his knees beside the
body of Sitting Bull, clutching his
bloody stomach. He gasps in pain.

Red Tomahawk and Shave Head enter,
holding Crow Foot.

RED TOMAHAWK
What shall we do with him?

BULLHEAD
He is the one who started all this. Do as you want.

They drag him, struggling, off stage.

CROW FOOT
Don't kill me, Uncles, don't kill me!

He keeps repeating this off stage until
we hear a gunshot, when we hear him no
more.

Bullhead falls dead.

Moments later McLaughlin enters stage
with Shave Head and Red Tomahawk right
behind. He observes the scene.

MCLAUGHLIN
Take Lieutenant Bullhead. He will be buried with full
military honors.

RED TOMAHAWK
And Sitting Bull?

MCLAUGHLIN
Choose a place hard to find. Bury him quickly. And deep.

> They each grab one of the dead men and
> drag them off stage.

> McLaughlin approaches the audience in
> order to speak directly.

MCLAUGHLIN
This cabin will rest as a place in honor of the brave
Indian police who made such a gallant and determined stand
in upholding the Government against their own race and
kindred.

> Walsh, Catherine Weldon and Buffalo
> Bill enter stage behind him to also
> address the audience, to McLaughlin's
> growing annoyance.

WALSH
I am glad to learn that Bull is relieved of his miseries
even if it took a bullet to do it. A man who wields such
power as Bull once did, that of a King, over a wild
spirited people cannot endure abject poverty, slavery and
beggary without suffering great mental pain and death is a
relief.

MCLAUGHLIN
Sitting Bull was an Indian of very mediocre ability, rather
dull, and much the inferior of Gall and others of his
lieutenants in intelligence.

CATHERINE
We were always good friends personally, but he hated
Christianity and found great satisfaction in taking my
converts back into heathendom while of course I felt great
satisfaction in converting his heathen friends.

WALSH

History does not tell us that a greater Indian than Bull
ever lived, he was the Mohammed of his people, the law and
king maker of the Sioux.

MCLAUGHLIN

He was pompous, vain, and boastful, and considered himself
a very important personage.

CATHERINE WELDON

I honored and respected Sitting Bull as if he was my own
father, and nothing can ever shake my faith in his good
qualities.

BUFFALO BILL

The greatest of all the Sioux in my time, or in any time
for that matter, was that wonderful old fighting man,
Sitting Bull, whose life will some day be written by a
historian who can really give him his due.

> Red Tomahawk and Shave Head have
> entered stage. McLaughlin has had
> enough.
>
> He motions to them and they
> discreetly but firmly indicate to
> Buffalo Bill, Walsh and Catherine
> Weldon to leave. They usher them off
> stage.
>
> From Off Stage McLaughlin now begins to
> hear the song Sitting Bull was wont to
> sing when his captivity began.
> (singing) I - ki - ci - ze wa-on kon he
> wa - na he - na - la ye - lo he i - yo -
> ti - ye ki - ya wa-on.
>
> McLaughlin is unnerved but carries on,
> addressing the audience with his views.

MCLAUGHLIN

The shot that killed him put a stop forever to the
domination of the ancien regime among the Sioux of the
Standing Rock Reservation. Sitting Bull never came to a
realizing sense of the necessity for accommodating himself

142

to the ways of the whites. I will go on to have a
distinguished career with the Indian Bureau. I will live a
long life and die in office. I'll write a book of memoirs
and call it My Friend the Indian.

With each phrase McLaughlin becomes
more and more unsettled, as if
haunted by the song and the singer
Sitting Bull who seems to have
escaped death and still lives. He
hurries off stage.

Curtain falls, but the song continues
a few moments longer to a peroration:
"I - ki - ci - ze wa-on kon he wa -
na he - na - la ye - lo he i - yo -
ti - ye ki - ya wa-on."

BUFFALO SOLDIER

A Play in Two Acts

Adapted from scenario
"RIGHT PROUD." THE BUFFALO SOLDIERS.

CAST

ZACH BURLEY--21. Angry, but does what he must.

HAL JONES--21-year-old farm boy. Brave and innocent.

HARRY "LUV" HARRIS--23. Goes through life with a smile.

SERGEANT MOSES STRONG--40. Veteran of war and slavery. A
    leader.

LADY BELLE--32. All of New Orleans gave her the name.

A BEAUTY--18. To die for.

Various young men and women.

All the characters in the play are black.

BUFFALO SOLDIER

ACT 1

CURTAIN RISES on a New Orleans
honkytonk in 1878. We are in mid
song.

Belting out a verse of "Camptown
Races" to beat hell is LADY BELLE.
She's singing with all the heart
she's got lots of, bouncing an
outrageous body she's got lots of,
too.

Acccompanying her is a young black
man, HARRY "LUV" HARRIS. His voice is
mellow, beautiful.

The audience loves it, shouting,
applauding, seconding. It is a black
group, an even mix of women and men,
who are there for LADY BELLE's
entertainment, maybe the best in New
Orleans.

A piano player provides the musical
accompaniment.

Lady Belle and Harris duo the last of
the song and it brings down the
house. APPLAUSE, SHOUTS, HUZZAHS.Lady
Annabelle hugs Harris, gives him a
big kiss on the cheek.

LADY BELLE
Lordy boy, you sure can sing. What s your name?

HARRIS
Harry Harris, but back home they call me "Luv."

LADY BELLE
Why's that?

He gives her smile she can't mistake,
bends down, tells it in her ear. Lady
Belle laughs, slaps him on the
shoulder.

LADY BELLE
Honey, round here sweet lovin' costs one dollar.

She moves off.

HARRIS
(yelling after her)
Well I ain't got it!

But hope resprings. He moves over to
a henna-haired beauty, starts sweet
talking her.

BURLEY and JONES enter. Jones is
dressed plainly, like the farm boy he
is. Burley is a farm boy too, but he
is garbed like a riverboat gambler in
a flashy vest and big white hat.

JONES
What're we doin' here, Zach?

BURLEY
It's your birthday.

JONES
We can't do any celebratin'.
We don't have jobs, we don't have prospects, and we sure as
hell ain't got any money.

BURLEY
(taking off his hat, massaging the felt)
Yet.

JONES
What'd you do, rob a riverboat?

BURLEY
Won it.

Burley smiles, shows a deck of cards
stashed in the bottom of the hat-
ruffles a few for Jones' benefit.

JONES

Didn't know you were that good.

BURLEY

I'm not. I'm lucky. Hal Jones, you're gonna' remember this
night for as long as you live. Watch me.

He heads over to a card table.
Importunes the gents there. They make
him a place.
Jones just shakes his head at his
friend's confidence. Eyes him
admiringly...but when a BEAUTY comes up
beside him, he passes to other
intentions.
He spends a long moment gathering
courage...when she smiles at him! Jones
is in heaven. He starts to say
something...and is abruptly elbowed
aside by Harris.

HARRIS

She's smilin' at me, brother.

JONES

You sure?

HARRIS

Watch me.

He leans over seductively to the
Beauty.

HARRIS

You believe in love?

BEAUTY

(nodding)
Uh-huh.

HARRIS

Love don't have nothing to do with money. It comes from the
heart.

                    BEAUTY
(nodding)
Uh-huh.

          He leans down, whispers in her ear.

                    BEAUTY
(shaking her head)
Huh-uh.

          She turns away in a huff.

                    JONES
Whatever you said, don't tell me.

                    HARRIS
I ain't through. They don't call me Sweet Lovin' 'cause of
that heifer on my Daddy's farm.

                    JONES
I ain't done it once, 'less you count--

                    HARRIS
Sheep and heifers.

                    JONES
(chuckling)
Naw...

                    HARRIS
Keep watchin' me.

                    JONES
Couldn't hardly go wrong here. All these ladies are so
pretty. And her...

          He means Lady Belle. She sashays by,
          turning heads and sparking dreams.

                    HARRIS
That's Lady Belle. This is her place. Every black man in New
Orleans'd like to watch the moonlight with her. You got about
as much chance--
(eyes him up and down for the first time)
Say, which bayou you from, boy?

                        JONES
How'd you know I was from the country?

                        HARRIS
(a beat)
Flipped a coin.

                    The Beauty turns back. Harris motions
                    for Jones to get lost.

                    Behind them, Burley lets out a WHOOP,
                    rakes in a pile of winnings. Jones
                    smiles, starts to move away...Suddenly
                    Lady Belle lets out a SHRIEK.

                    SERGEANT STRONG enters. Wearing the
                    distinctive blue and yellow of the 9th
                    U.S. Cavalry, hat too, he's an
                    impressive figure and it's no wonder he
                    creates a wide swath of attention.The
                    girls in Lady Belle's flock toward
                    him...including Harris' Beauty, who
                    hangs him out to dry.

                        HARRIS
Hey!

                    Jones looks excited as Lady Belle
                    grandly greets the Sergeant.

                        LADY BELLE
A beer for the Buffalo Soldier!

                    SQUEALS and giggles from the girls.
                    Lady Belle greets the sergeant with
                    flamboyant hugs and kisses.

                        LADY BELLE
You've been away too long.
(to the crowd)
Look how he's thinned out.

                        STRONG
Been livin' on lizards and horse piss.

The piano player hands the sergeant a
mug of beer. He seizes it gratefully,
almost downs it all in one huge gulp--a
feat that brings oohs and ahs from the
crowd gathered around.

                    JONES
Damn...

Harris elbows his way in to the group,
so as to be closer to the Beauty who
left him in the lurch. She is his focus
of attention, not the soldier.

                    HARRIS
Come on, honey, forget Sergeant Lizard.

Before she can answer Jones directs a
question toward the sergeant.

                    JONES
Excuse me sir... What's a Buffalo Soldier?

Strong mocks disgust. He BANGS the
empty beer mug down on a table. The
SOUND brings the music to a halt.

                    STRONG
Hear that, Belle? What'd I tell you? These boys
shoulda stayed in the cottonfields.
          (striding forward,
          looking at the lot)
Hell, I bet they ain't even heard of emancipation.
They ain't workin'. I can tell that.

                    JONES
          I'm lookin'.

Strong confronts him.

                    STRONG
Yeah. At the shoeshine stands. At the stable, shoveling shit
around. (sticking his nose in Jones' face)
Sharecroppin'...workin' like a mule and getting treated a
whole lot worse--you hear what I'm sayin', boy?

The chastened Jones nods. Strong
circles around his now rapt audience.
Jones is listening to all this
intently.

STRONG

'Course. . . you want to earn
$13 a month in the U.S. Cavalry......

Gasps from the crowd at this enormous
sum.

STRONG

Buffalo's a sacred animal to the Indians. Some say they call
us "Buffalo Soldiers" cause of our hair.
(tweaking one of his locks)
Others say it's respect.
'Cause of how we fight.
We do the job. We earn our money. And a whole lot more...
Satisfaction. Honor.
(fierce conviction)
Pride.

In b.g. Burley rakes in the biggest pot
of all. The others give up; he's too
lucky. They get up from the table.

STRONG

(to Jones)
You all want to know what a Buffalo Soldier is? Find out for
yourself...come to
Jackson Square Recruiting Station tomorrow. I'll be there.
Waitin' to see who wants to live for something bigger than
hisself.

Burley comes up to Jones. Waving a pile
of cash.

BURLEY

Look at that! Told you I was lucky, didn't I?
(looking around at the girls)
So what do you like?

JONES

Them uniforms.

BURLEY

Say what?

Jones steps forward.

JONES

(to Strong)
Sir....I'm with you.

The crowd buzzes. Some APPLAUSE,
huzzahs for Jones as Strong vigorously
shakes his hand.

JONES

Ready to sign up right now, Sergeant.!

Strong is distracted. He has noticed
that the Beauty who was Harris' quarry
is staring at him with misty doe eyes-
and she isn't the only one.

STRONG

Er...no, tomorrow morn--afternoon's just fine.
Yeah, first thing tomorrow afternoon. I like your attitude,
son.

Strong shakes Jones' hand again, then
quickly turns his attention to the
Beauty. He circles his arm around her
and she's glad. Harris is aghast.

Burley looks stunned by his friend's
decision.

BURLEY

You gone crazy?

JONES

Think about it. Black men in the United States Cavalry.

BURLEY

Lot of black men in Hades, too, but we don't got to go there.

JONES

Join up with me. We'll ride together, fight together.

BURLEY
Yeah, and my mama raised an idjit son.
(shakes his head)
You need some educating. Right quick.

>He moves over, begins an earnest
>conversation with Lady Belle. He waves
>his newly won cash to punctuate the
>discussion.

>Harris is still fit to be tied, but the
>Sergeant is frying other fish than his
>Beauty at the moment. He seizes the
>chance to sidle over to her and ask:

HARRIS
(to the Beauty)
How come he gets the la-dee-da?

BEAUTY
Honey, he's a hero.

HARRIS
(loudly)
Count me in, sergeant!

HARRIS
(emphatically)
Buffalo Soldiers, yeah!

>Squeals of admiration from several of
>the girls. The Beauty looks at Harris
>with new eyes. He's glad. Jones is
>still watching the sergeant admiringly
>as Burley comes up.

JONES
I sure do like those uniforms.

>Burley takes him by the shoulder.

BURLEY
Coupla' minutes from now you won't be thinkin' about nothin'
higher'n your belly button.
Jones my friend--

He wheels him around. There, hands on hips, smiling with a smile as wide as the Mississippi, is Lady Belle.

BURLEY
--you are about to become a man.

He shoves him forward. Jones starts walking toward Lady Belle. He walks like a hypnotic, riveted.

BURLEY
Happy birthday.

Harris sees it all. Happy for his new friend, he signals to the rest of the crowd, then launches into a verse of "Camptown Races." Charged by his wonderful voice, they join in. As Jones walks toward Lady Belle, her wide smile and his manhood, awed and ecstatic at the prospect before him, almost the whole honkytonk is singing:

HARRIS AND GROUP
'Gwine to run all night,
'Gwine to run all day,
I bet my money on the bobtail nag,
Somebody bet on the bay.

CURTAIN

ACT 2

CURTAIN RISES on the Arizona desert.

Scrub and sand and barren rock.

Burley enters, supporting the wounded
Jones by the shoulders. He lays him
down gently on the sand, back against
a small boulder so he is almost
sitting. Jones' cavalry jacket is
soaked with his blood.

Jones grimaces with each movement. He
is clutching his stomach where a
gaping wound has bled profusely.

Sergeant Strong enters, backing
toward them to provide cover. His
rifle is poised, he eyes the desert
OFF.

All the men's uniforms are dusty,
caked with sand and dirt and alkali.

They've been through hell and it
shows.

                    STRONG
How many you count?

                    BURLEY
A good dozen I'd say.

                    STRONG
We did some damage. I counted
three on the ground, sure.

                    BURLEY
Think I nicked another one...he was riding side of his
horse.

                    STRONG
Old Comanchero trick. Warned you about that.

            Harris enters from Stage Left
            opposite them. He carries a rifle
            too, holds it warily like Strong.

                    STRONG
See anything?

                    HARRIS
Dust. They're headin' off to the South.

                    STSTRONG
Mexico. We ride like hell we just might--

            He hesitates, looks down at the wounded
            Jones.

                    JONES
Ain't nothing, Sergeant. Patch me up and let's go.

            Strong lowers his rifle, kneels down
            beside Jones to inspect the wound. He
            motions to Burley and together they
            remove Jones' jacket. Harris hovers
            over them, watching.

                    STRONG
Took you a long time to tell me you were hit.

160

JONES

Yessir. We was making real good time. Didn't want
to slow us down.

STRONG

Un-huh. Let's hope your stomach's stouter
than your head.

JONES

I got suckered.

BURLEY

You surely did.

JONES

Played like he was dead. I shouldn't have followed him up
that draw.

BURLEY

Hadn't been you it'd have been me.

Jones squirms a little as Strong
checks the wound. The sergeant doesn't like
what he sees.

JONES

He rides a bay sorrel. Big man, carries a warclub. Next
time he's mine. Won't fool me again, no way. Went and got
myself shot, bunky. Guess I ain't much of a soldier.

BURLEY

Hey, name me a good soldier ain't been nicked.

STRONG

Way you drew their fire, hadn't been for you we'd all be
singing Glory Hallelujah. You did fine, son, real fine.

HARRIS

I'm gonna recommend you for a
medal.

JONES

Aw, nobody's gonna give a honor like that to a black
man.

HARRIS

It's happened.

JONES

What you doin' with this patrol anyway? I thought you was
tryin' to be the Major's aide-de camp. So you could stay in
camp.

HARRIS

I was. I told the Major I'd be the best aide he ever aided.
First thing, he asked me to give him a shave. Major said,
way I used a razor, U.S. Cavalry officers would be safer if
I was in the field.

> Jones laughs. The others smile, even
> Burley.

JONES

Never could figure why you joined the Cavalry anyway, Luv.
Man of your experience. (chuckles)

HARRIS

Well, I was told the women out here looked like angels and
loved like devils. I'd have to beg them to stop.

STRONG

What damn fool told you that?

HARRIS

You, sir.
(to Strong's glare)
You'd had a few beers.

> They laugh. But this time Jones chokes
> a little on his blood. Coughs. Strong
> gets Jones' shirt open and for the
> first time they see Jones' wound. The
> sight hits all of them hard. Strong
> leans back on his heels.

JONES

I don't feel the pain no more. That's good, ain't it?

> None of them can find the words to
> answer.

JONES

Leave him to me, understand? Next time he's mine. You hear
me, Zach?

BURLEY
(swallowing hard, softly, to Jones)
Understood.

> Strong motions to Burley who hands him
> Jones' jacket.

STRONG
Hold this tight. Maybe...stop the blood.

> Jones clutches it hard over the wound.
> Burley moves away to the edge of the
> stage. His face is grim with anger. He
> holds his rifle high, waves it at the
> vanished enemy.

BURLEY
Comancheros!
(his shout is lost in the winds)
Comancheros!

> No answer. He aims his rifle, fires a shot.
> The sound is harsh, shocking.

BURLEY
Come out and fight! Here I am!

> Strong leaves Harris with Jones, comes
> over, grabs him by the shoulder.

STRONG
You're fightin' the wind, boy.

> Burley turns, confronts Strong.

BURLEY
Might as well. Hardtack crackers taste like sand. Food's got
weevils. Horses so scrawny... Only thing works fine is the
bullets. What are we fighting for, Sergeant? Huh? Why are we
getting ourselves killed? It's not for respect. These people
don't care about us. We could bring their heads in on a
stick, know what they'd say? "Good work boy, now here, clean
my shithouse." Where's the pride in that, sergeant?

                    STRONG
Let me tell you something. Sure they send us into hell, but
it's not just 'cause we're black. It's cause we're good. We got
guts and we show it when it comes time
to live or die. The only time thét counts. And I'll tell you
another thing. Bad as it gets, it's better than what we came
from. You want respect, you got to deserve it. Jones don't care
what those people think. His pride comes from inside, where it
should. He's a brave man. Did his duty. Some day I promise
you, that's what they'll remember.

                    BURLEY
You really believe that, Sergeant?

                    STRONG
Yes sir, I do.

                    JONES
(calling over) Hey, Zach. Know what I'd like?

                    BURLEY
What's that, Hal?

                    JONES
A little water. Tongue's dry as this dust.

                    BURLEY
You got it.

                    Burley starts to move over to him.
                    Strong grabs his shoulder.

                    STRONG
We still got a desert to cross.

                    BURLEY
He's like a little brother to me. I was always there, helping
him out of trouble. Wasn't any way I could keep him out of
the Army, though. He was on fire. All I could do was tag
along, like a good big brother, watching out for him.
(a beat) Some job I did.

                    He shakes off Strong's hand, moves over
                    to Jones. He unstraps his canteen from
                    his waist, shakes it. The sound is
                    negligible, indicating the canteen is
                    almost empty.

Harris comes up to him. He holds his
own canteen, pours a few precious drops
of his water into Burley's.

BURLEY
Got you a drink, Hal.

He bends down but Sergeant Strong stops
him.

Holding out his canteen. Burley looks
surprised.

Strong adds his contribution of water.

Burley puts the canteen to Jones'
mouth. He takes it gratefully.

Jones finishes the drink, smacks his
lips.

JONES
That was good. Thanks.
Your voice still work, Luv?

HARRIS
I reckon.

JONES
Like to hear it. Sing me a song 'bout the Glory Land.

HARRIS
You got it.

Harris pauses for just a moment, then
begins his song.

HARRIS
(sings)
"Well I looked over Jordan--"

--but his voice breaks. He can't
continue. Jones is relaxed in reverie
and doesn't seem to notice.

JONES

He sings good. Better than the
angels. Right now the Lord's looking down and saying, son,
hang on till we hear that boy sing. Well all right. All
right. (looking down, feeling the cloth) Sure messed up this
uniform. Reckon I can get another?

BURLEY

(fighting his emotions)
Whatever you want, soldier.

JONES

I'm right proud of it.
(assured, Jones leans back, his eyes open, staring toward
the sky)
Right proud.

He says no more.

HARRIS finds his voice.

HARRIS

(singing)
Well I looked over Jordan
And what did I see,
Comin' boy to carry me home,
A band of angels comin' after me,
Comin' boy to carry me home.

Strong takes the jacket from the dead
man's hands and lays it over his
face. Strong and Burley bow their heads as
Harris' song rises richly melodious
toward the heavens.

HARRIS

(singing)
Swing low, sweet chariot,
Comin' boy to carry me home,
Swing low, sweet chariot,
Comin' boy to carry me home.

CURTAIN.

Martin Copeland is a screenwriter, playwright and author of two novels, THE BOYS FROM DOGTOWN and LA LOVE STORIES.